Idaho Fall

A twisty whodunit

D.J. Maughan

Hulyeseg Inc

For you, Laurie. From the first time you welcomed me into your home as a sixteen-year-old kid, you made me feel part of the family. You are a wonderful example of love, kindness, and compassion. Thank you for being the best mother-in-law a man could have. I love you!

Chapter 1

Rita

The cost: $2.27 million. Not pesos. Dollars. Good old Uncle Sam American currency. That's what I paid for this house only six months ago. The median home value in Idaho Falls is $425,000. This means that I paid $1.845 million more than almost all the other twenty thousand homeowners in the area.

All that money, yet the simplest thing doesn't work. I mash the garage door opener harder this time, digging my nail into it. Nothing happens. I grit my teeth and push open the driver's side door of my Mercedez Benz S class.

Aside from the smattering of outdoor lights adorning the brick structure, the house is dark. I walk down the driveway and up the steps leading to the front door, my tennis shoes silent on the newly formed concrete.

I peer through the expansive custom iron door window at the entrance. It's dark. Not a light on inside. I curse and pull on the door handle. Nothing happens. I press the handle, squeezing the latch. It doesn't give. Muttering, I bang on the door. Silence. I reach inside the jacket of my coat but feel nothing. It's empty. I turn back and look at the beam of headlights and exhaust streaming from my car. When I exited the gym fifteen minutes ago, my heart was pumping so hard I could barely bring myself to wrap my jacket around me. Now, with the coolness of the morning and dampness of my clothing, I can feel the nip of the air biting my skin. It does little to help my mood.

Before turning back to the car, I reach over and press the button on the video doorbell. A chime sounds, and the ring around the button lights up and dances with flashing lights in a clockwise direction. Echoing within the house, I can hear our speaker system announce, "Someone is at the front door."

That does the trick. The large chandelier hanging in our entrance bursts to life. I can see my husband, James, coming down the stairs. He's wearing his normal bedtime attire—sweatpants and a white T-shirt. When he reaches the front door, he looks out, trying to determine who might ring the doorbell this early in the morning. He sees me, and I can tell from the blurriness in his eyes, I've wakened him. No surprise there, his laziness is a constant point of frustration. He unlocks the door, and I push it open as he pulls. I'm so angry I brush past him, shaking my head, my ponytail flipping from side to side.

"What time is it?" he asks, rubbing his eyes. Like always, he's oblivious to my emotions. "Did you forget something?"

I turn back to glare at him as I continue down the hallway to the garage. I can hear him trailing after me. I open the door, push the button on the wall, and slam the door in his face as I descend the stairs and walk toward the car. When I reach it, I shift into drive and enter the garage. James stands at the opening of the house, watching me. I press the button on the vehicle and watch with frustration in the rearview mirror. Nothing happens. It doesn't work.

"What's with you?" he asks as I exit the car and walk toward him.

I glare at him, shake my head, and look away.

"What?"

"What time is it, James?" I ask.

He shrugs. "I don't know."

Exactly. "Are any of them awake?"

I needn't have asked. His silence says it all.

"It's already seven ten. David's going to be late, again... Donovan too. If they get one more tardy, they'll be marked 'unsatisfactory.' Do you know what that means? They'll have to pay a fine and do makeup work or they won't graduate."

I brush past him in the doorframe, and he mutters something.

"What?" I ask, flipping around. I'm challenging him with my eyes, daring him to repeat it. I'm at least a head shorter, and probably a hundred pounds lighter, but he knows better than to say what's on his mind and looks away. I watch him, my eyes smoldering, then turn away and walk down the stairs to the basement.

Everyone knows about a new-car smell. That smell lingers in a new vehicle after purchase but eventually fades the more it's driven. New houses have a new-home smell. It's different from the car, but no less potent. Maybe it's the fresh paint or the new carpet and flooring. Maybe a combination of everything. Our house still has it.

We have four sons. The two oldest, David and Donovan, have bedrooms downstairs. The two youngest, Gilbert and Reed, share the upstairs with us. Our home is a large, modern, two-story structure with an acre of land behind it.

I flip on the lights on the stairway, cross the large family room, and reach my oldest son's bedroom door. I don't bother to knock and push it open. The smell of teenage boy overwhelms me. It's a mixture of body odor, sweaty feet, and rotting food. I flip on the light, and he jerks in the bed. His phone rests on the nightstand beside him. It's buzzing and lighting up.

"David, get up!" I shout. "You're late."

He groans, and one eye opens, his thick, brown hair matted on his head. He turns away from me toward the wall. I walk across the room, grip the covers, and pull them down. He jerks again and turns his head back toward me.

"What's your problem?" he says without opening his eyes.

"You can't be late again. If you're late, you'll have a *U*."

"So?"

I glare at him, but he doesn't see it. His eyes are still closed.

"David... get up."

He opens one eye, blinking against the light. He's wearing nothing but black underwear. A smattering of body hair around his nipples and on his stomach. He's a big kid, as big as his father, and recently I can't stop from wondering how I pushed him out of my body seventeen years ago.

Seeing I won't back down, he pushes up from the bed. "Fine." He walks past me toward the bathroom and shuts the door.

I step to it. "And the shower has to be short. You can't be in there over two minutes."

He speaks, but not to me. He tells the speaker system to play a band I've never heard of, and loud rap music blares. I exhale, shake my head, and leave his room. I cross the basement and approach my second son's bedroom door. I'm about to barge in, but stop when I see light emanating from below. I knock, pause, then enter, not wanting to see another naked teenage boy.

Donovan sits on his bed, fully clothed, staring at his phone. His backpack lies beside him. He looks as ready as he can. Only his shoes are missing. His glasses are crooked, and one pant leg is tucked into his sock. I enter the room, but he's still not looking at me.

"Donovan?"

He turns, startled. "Hey, Mom."

"What's with this room?"

"What?"

"Look at it," I say, demonstrating with my hand toward the floor. "Why can't you clean up after yourself? Look at this. You can't even see the carpet."

It's true. The floor is covered with clothes. It seems every piece of clothing he's ever owned adorns it. He has no idea what's clean and what's dirty.

He looks at me, then the floor, then back at me. "Sorry," he says and looks down.

I sigh and shake my head. "Are you ready to go?"

"Almost."

"Okay. Well, get your shoes on and come upstairs. David's not ready yet, so you can eat something before you go. And I want this room cleaned up after school or no video games."

He nods, and I exit the room. I walk back to the bathroom door and hear the shower running. David's singing at the top of his lungs to a song I've never heard. It's off-key and sounds terrible.

"David! Shut off the water and get dressed. You have to leave in five minutes!"

He doesn't reply, so I bang on the door. The water turns off, and I can hear him moving around. After a few seconds, the bathroom door opens, and he jumps when he sees me standing there, arms crossed.

"Gosh, Rita. Take a chill pill."

I hate it when he calls me Rita, which seems to be all the time now. "You have three minutes," I say.

He's wearing only a towel around his waist and walks past me into his room. He drops the towel, exposing his naked butt. He turns his neck and smiles a "kiss it" smile.

I throw my hands in the air, shake my head, and walk up the stairs. I enter the kitchen and see my three youngest boys sitting at the bar. Donovan followed my instructions and came up to eat breakfast with his younger brothers.

Our kitchen features a large quartz island with six barstools scattered across one side. James stands at the sink; he's now wearing a dark hoodie and sweatpants. Gilbert, my second youngest, sees me and swivels away from his Life cereal.

"Hi, Mom."

"Hi," I say grumpily and cross my arms, looking at all of them. "You know, I want you to understand something. I can't do everything in this house. I work so hard every day, providing all this. I can't be responsible for all of you too. I need you guys to take some responsibility. I need you to help."

James turns from the sink, and we look at each other, but he says nothing. I'm talking mostly to him, and he knows it. Behind me, David ascends the stairs. He never enters the kitchen, instead turning toward the hallway and front door, his backpack slung over his shoulder.

"Donovan," I say, "go with your brother."

Donovan gives me a "Why me?" look, takes another spoonful of his Fruit Loops, and grabs his backpack, running after his brother. David reaches the front door, and I can see he's got white earbuds in his ears. I walk down the hall after them to watch from the front room window as they climb into the old Toyota Camry James had once used as his commuter car.

James's deep voice coming from the kitchen pulls me away from the window.

"Come on, boys, let's go. We're carpooling today."

Gilbert is in his second year of junior high, and Reed is in his first. I leave the front room and head them off as they reach the door to the garage. I reach out and hug Reed. My baby with blond hair and green eyes is almost as tall as me now. I wish him a good day, and Gilbert wraps an arm around my shoulder. He passed me in height a couple of months ago. It won't be long before he towers over me like his big brothers.

"Bye, Mom," Gilbert says, and the two boys walk down the stairs to the Tahoe, looking at their phones as they go.

I feel James beside me before I turn around. We look at each other, and he says, "Sorry." He keeps his distance, making no effort to touch me. He shrugs and half smiles. "What can I say? I like my sleep. I guess that's where David gets it."

He's trying to pass it off as no big deal, but I hear it as just another excuse. Why can't he shut up and own his mistakes? We stare at each other, the two feet between us feeling farther with every passing day.

For years, we were happy. I should say, *he* was happy. I was the mother at home, raising the children, running the kids to school, and volunteering in the classroom. He was the husband hustling off to work every morning, late. Life was hectic, and money was tight. Nothing like going to the grocery store praying your card works when you checkout. The embarrassment when it didn't.

It was on a day like that when inspiration struck. Frustrated with my life and looking for more, I stared at myself in the mirror. My hair didn't have any gray yet, and wrinkles had yet to appear around the corners of my eyes, but lumps appeared under my clothing. The toll of carrying four babies inside of me for nine months was visible. I was a mom now. Men no longer gave me a passing glance. I dreamed of a nonsurgical solution. Something that a common woman, like me, could afford. What if clothing could accentuate your assets while minimizing your flaws? I got out the sewing machine I was so accustomed to using to mend and fix the boys' clothes, making them last just a few months longer until they outgrew them. I worked for weeks, day and night, taking advantage of any minute I could find in the day. I was obsessed. Finally, after countless hours, I had it. It was a bodysuit I wore under my clothing. It did exactly what I wanted.

My body was mine again, like it had been before the stretch marks and nursing.

I began wearing it under everything. I knew it worked; James couldn't keep his eyes off me. I caught men checking me out. It fit with any outfit. I felt young and confident, and other women were noticing too. Before I knew it, my friends were asking if I was going to a trainer or on some special diet. They asked if I could make them one. I was getting so many orders I couldn't keep up. That's when my clothing line, BEAU, was born.

"I can't be the one to wake them every morning, James. You're the adult. David and Donovan are in high school now."

His jaw sets. "Exactly. They should be able to get themselves up. It shouldn't be up to me all the time."

I fight to control my voice. "And what else do you have to do? You don't work. They follow your example. You expect teenage boys to get up when you can't even get yourself up?"

He glares down at me, then walks past, raising his hand in an "I give up" gesture. He descends the stairs, gets in the car, and starts it up. I step forward, but he's reversing out of the garage without so much as a glance back. I shake my head and close the door. I lean against it, enjoying the silence but angry with yet another fight, when I look down at my watch. It's two minutes to eight, and I've got a video call in two minutes. I rush into the kitchen, pour a cup of coffee, and run up the stairs to our bedroom. I grab my laptop from beside the bed, put my coffee on the nightstand, and walk toward the double doors that open onto the balcony overlooking the back of our house, my de facto office. I love this spot, especially on days like today.

The balcony opens to the west. In the mornings, the sun rises behind the house, casting a blanket of light on the view in front of me. The mountain range in the far distance makes me feel comfortable and familiar.

I hold the laptop in one arm while typing my password with the other. When I reach the balcony, my foot slips, and I lose control. The laptop flies forward, and I react by stretching to catch it before it falls. It's a mistake. I know it immediately, but it's too late. I catch the laptop just in time for my body to slam into the short railing at the edge of the balcony. I almost go over but stop myself. I look down, blowing out air in relief. That was stupid. If I had gone over the edge, it might have killed me. It's a long way down to the patio. A movement catches my eye, and I turn to see someone coming toward me. The face is hidden beneath a black hoodie, but I know exactly who it is. The figure pushes me, and my momentum is too great now. I can't stop it. I flip over the rail, arms and legs flailing as the blue sky and sun's rays pass further from me. After twenty feet, I strike the composite wood surface with a loud thump, and everything goes black.

Chapter 2

I don't quite know how to describe it. It's not like I opened my eyes and suddenly became aware of my consciousness. I don't even have eyes. At least, I don't think I do. I don't have shape. I just...am. I don't have physical constraints, but something is pulling me. It's not above me. There's not a cloud in the sky. Only a massive shade of blue and the sun. The sun lights the area all around me, but I can't feel its warmth. Although the colors are vibrant and intoxicating, it's no more potent than a lightbulb. It's not the sky above that calls to me. It's something on the ground. Some gravitational pull.

I look down and see a body. It's a woman. Her legs and arms are spread. She's lying on her back. Her brown hair with blonde highlights is pulled back in a ponytail. Only a portion of it is visible under her head. As I examine her, my consciousness moves closer. Her skin is pale, lifeless. A ripple like a cool breeze flows over me as I approach. Her eyes are shut. She looks as if she's asleep. She's wearing a bright-pink long-sleeve shirt, black leggings, and bright-pink tennis shoes. A logo of a *B* is embroidered on the left side of her chest. Something's wrong.

Beneath her, on the deck surface, pools a crimson liquid. She shouldn't be here. Something happened to her. As I search for the origin of the crimson liquid, a sound from within the house grabs my attention. I move away from the body. Inside the house, a man enters the kitchen. He pours himself a cup of coffee. He exits the kitchen and ascends the stairs. I follow him as he enters the large bedroom. I know him. I recognize him, as if he's someone close to me. The blankets on the bed are disheveled. He moves toward the bathroom but stops. Taking a sip of his coffee, he looks at the coffee cup on the nightstand beside the bed. He walks over to it. Seeing it full, he turns and looks to the balcony. His expression changes, and he walks toward it.

When he reaches the threshold, he stops.

"Rita?" he calls, looking around. "Rita?"

Rita? Is that the woman on the ground?

He steps out onto the balcony and nearly slips, gripping the railing. The railing is low, only reaching partway up his thigh. He looks down. "Rita!" he screams when he sees her. He drops his coffee cup and sprints through the room and down the stairs. He runs out the back of the house to the patio deck.

"Rita!"

The woman doesn't respond or move. He kneels beside her, reaching out tentatively, then stops.

"Rita," he calls, but she doesn't react. I can see the source of the crimson liquid now. The back of her hair is matted with blood. It pools on the surface and drips down.

The man calls to her one more time, then backs away and runs into the house. He picks up the phone on the counter and dials 9-1-1.

Chapter 3
Hank and Joyce

"Who sings this song?"

Hank looks over at Joyce, his partner, from the driver's side of the white Dodge Charger he's driving. She's looking out the window, lost in thought, unaware she's asked the question. He knows better. She does nothing by accident. He turns up the radio and listens more intently.

Razzle 'n' a dazzle 'n' a flash a little light
Television lover, baby, go all night
Sometime, anytime, sugar me sweet
Little miss innocent sugar me, yeah
So c'mon, take a bottle, shake it up
Break the bubble, break it up
Pour some sugar on me
Ooh, in the name of love
Pour some sugar on me
C'mon, fire me up
Pour your sugar on me
I can't get enough

"Aerosmith?"

She turns and watches him, a smile playing at the corners of her mouth. "Final answer?"

The smile stops him. After hearing the chorus, he felt so confident. But now... He holds up a finger.

It's a game Joyce loves to play. From the first day he was assigned to partner with the legendary Joyce Powers, she's been quizzing him. After receiving the partnership assignment from the captain after his promotion to detective, Hank had trailed her as they'd walked out of the station and headed for the car. She had tossed him the keys, saying nothing. Not two blocks into the commute, she'd turned up the radio, looked out the window, and asked him to identify the song artist. He'd stared at her, and she'd smiled at him like she was now.

"Tell you what," she'd said, "you get it right, and I'll buy you a Coke. Get it wrong...and you buy me one. Deal?"

Knowing he was being set up, but worrying he would disappoint her, Hank agreed. He bought her a Coke that day and almost every day since.

"No...wait. It's Def Leppard."

Her smile vanishes. "Final answer?"

"Yes." He says it with more conviction than he feels.

Joyce nods. "Correct."

"Ha!" Hank exclaims, slapping the steering wheel.

She grins and goes back to looking out the window. "Well done, Detective."

It's the *detective* that pulls his attention from the road. He nearly swerves as he looks at her. He was pleased that, for the first time in weeks, she'd be buying rather than him. But her calling him "detective" fills him with pride. *Detective* is a term Joyce reserves for excellence. This was only the third time she'd used it when speaking of him. Three times in the nine months since they became partners. The other two were crime scene investigations. He had noticed something she had missed. Or, perhaps, she was testing him and he'd passed.

Aware that his eyes are on her, she doesn't look at him. "I think this is it," she says, pointing to the corner store on the right. He pulls the vehicle into one of the twenty open parking spaces and they exit. A balding man, medium height, lean, mid forties, is standing outside waiting for them.

"Mr. Decker?" Joyce asks, extending her hand to him after exiting the vehicle. "My name is Detective Joyce Powers, and this is my partner, Hank Gardener. I understand you've had a robbery?"

Mr. Decker peers at Joyce and then up at Hank. Walter Matthau and Jack Lemon were a less odd pairing than these two. Joyce had been on the force for thirty years. She was less than a year from retirement. She was small, below five feet, white, with short, graying hair. She looked more like a character from *The Golden Girls* than a detective.

Hank, on the other hand, had been on the force for less than a year. Joyce was his first partner and trainer. A California native, he came to Idaho to play college football as a defensive tackle at Boise State. After a tryout in the NFL, he returned to Idaho and never left. Six foot five, two hundred and seventy pounds, and black. He was a man who garnered a lot of attention. Especially in lily-white southern Idaho.

"Mr. Decker? The robbery?" Joyce prods.

Decker shakes his head, lost in thought, and turns his attention back to her.

"Let me show you."

He walks them through the store, past the racks of road and mountain bikes, to the back. A couple of young kids in their early twenties watch them. They have bicycles before them on stands, tires removed, and tools in their hands. There's a door behind the maintenance area. It's propped on the doorframe and removed from the hinges.

"When I came in this morning, I found it this way."

Both detectives nod, and Hank moves over to examine the door more closely.

"Sir, do you have a security system in the store?"

Decker shakes his head. "I've never needed one."

Hank holds a notepad and makes a note.

"Security cameras? Nothing? I saw a sign out front," Joyce says.

"Well, yeah, there's a camera, but it doesn't store recordings. It notifies me of motion, but I shut off the notifications on my phone. They used to wake me up at night with a cat or raccoon walking past."

"I see."

Hank takes a couple of giant strides and is back beside Joyce. Decker looks at him and takes a step back.

"What did they take?" Joyce asks.

Decker walks them back out to the retail section of the building. "They took two bikes," he says as they walk.

"Only two?"

He nods.

They reach the west wall, and a bike mount sits empty.

"They must have known what they were doing?"

"What makes you say that?" Joyce asks.

"Because they took the most expensive bikes in the store."

Joyce examines the bike on the ground below the mount on the wall. "Maybe," she says.

"Oh, believe me," Decker says, raising his voice, frustration showing. Hank glares at him, and he ducks his head and goes on more calmly. "They know bikes. This one was a Santa Cruz Heckler. And the other one," Decker points to another mount on the opposite wall, "was a Pivot Mach 4. They knew bikes."

Joyce looks at him, then at Hank, then back to Decker. "I haven't ridden a bike in," Joyce pauses and blows out her breath, "maybe twenty years. I don't know the first thing about them. Would you believe that?"

Decker grunts and nods.

"But I would have stolen the same bikes if I could only take two."

Decker guffaws. "No, you wouldn't."

"I would, actually."

Decker rolls his eyes and then glances at Hank. Hank says nothing, his eyes trained on him.

"You don't believe me?"

Decker smiles and shakes his head.

"Just look at your store, Mr. Decker. I'm betting you've owned it for quite a while."

"Thirteen years."

Joyce nods. "And you're a smart businessman. Maybe short-sighted, turning off notifications about camera activity and storage notwithstanding."

Hank smiles.

"But I'm betting you know you have the highest margins on the two stolen bikes. That's why you placed them above the others on a mount. Look around. They're the only two mounts in this place."

Decker frowns.

"They aren't just more expensive than the others. You make more money when you sell one. You're placing a premium on the bikes. What does each cost? Twenty thousand?"

Decker's eyebrows shoot up in surprise. "How'd you know that?"

Joyce doesn't answer. "And you make...maybe seven thousand on each?"

Shock registers in Decker's eyes, and Hank's smile widens.

"But I will agree with you on one thing, Mr. Decker."

Deckers's tone is soft now. "Oh?"

Joyce nods. "Your thieves, more than likely, knew bikes."

Decker's face contorts with confusion.

"They only took two. If I were a common thief, I'd bring a truck and load up. Those aren't the only bikes with value. That leads me to believe they had a limited capacity. A bike rack in their vehicle. They took two because they could only carry two."

"So what does that mean?"

She ignores the question. "Are you familiar with insurance fraud, Mr. Decker?"

Fury fills his eyes. "What are you suggesting?" He takes a step toward Joyce but quickly looks up as Hank moves between them.

"I'm not suggesting anything. I'm telling you that you stole the bikes, hoping to be paid insurance money. Judging by the dust built up on the stands, you held those bikes for months. They've been eating up your cash flow."

Five minutes later, Joyce and Hank climb back in the car, and Hank pulls out onto the road. He looks at her, but she's staring out the window. She glances over at him as he drives to their favorite gas station.

"Double or nothing?" She points to the radio on the dash.

Hank shakes his head.

"No?"

"Nope."

"Why not?"

"Because I don't want two Cokes."

She laughs, and he grins at her.

"How did you know, anyway?"

"What?"

"How much the guy made on each bike? How did you know?"

She goes back to looking out the window and waves a hand. "Oh, that..."

"Yeah. I mean, I understand how you knew their worth. At least a ballpark. Each bike had a price tag. But how'd you know how much he made on them?"

She turns back to him and smiles when her phone rings. She takes it out of the carrier she wears on her belt, checks the ID, and answers. "Yes, Chief."

Hank can hear the low voice of the police captain on the other end of the line, but he can't make out the words. Joyce pulls out her notepad and writes an address. She repeats it into the phone, then hangs up.

"Looks like the Coke will have to wait."

Chapter 4

Rita

The broken woman on the patio is me! I'm the one who fell.

The man remained on the phone with the operator until the emergency personnel arrived. A woman in a uniform escorted him away from the body to the kitchen and sat him in a chair facing away from the rear of the house while they worked on the woman. After sitting, he looked at the floor, rocking slightly from side to side.

"Is she your wife?" the woman asks.

As if the mention of the injured woman brings back his memory, he turns and stands. The woman comes forward and gently pushes him back down to the chair.

"Sir, the best thing you can do right now is focus and answer my questions."

The man stares blankly at her.

"Sir, are you hearing me? Is she your wife?"

"Umm...yes."

The woman nods and writes on the sheet attached to a clipboard. "What's your name?"

"James."

"James, I'm Carol. What's your last name?"

"Burch."

"Okay, thank you, James. And your wife? What's her name?"

He was staring at his hands, but the mention of her brings his head back around. He leans to the side, trying to see as the emergency personnel work on her.

"Is she going to be alright?"

"James?" The woman touches his shoulder and waves at him until he looks back and makes eye contact. "James, I need you to focus on me. I have some important questions to ask you. The best thing you can do for your wife right now is to answer my questions. Okay? Are you with me, James?" His eyes focus and she nods. "Great. James, what's your wife's name?"

"Rita."

"Rita Burch?"

"Yes."

"And how old is she?"

"Forty-one."

"Date of birth?"

James narrows his eyes in concentration. A wrinkle forms on his forehead. "May thirty, nineteen eighty-three."

"Is your wife allergic to any medication?"

"Huh?"

"Rita, is she allergic to anything?"

"Not that I know of."

She nods and makes a note. "Do you have insurance?"

"Yes."

"Do you know who the provider is?"

"Blue Cross."

"Thank you. James, can you tell me what happened?"

James shakes his head, and it resembles the shaking in his hands. "I don't know. I took our kids to school, and when I came home, she was lying there. I think she fell off the balcony."

"And what time did you leave the house to take the kids?"

"About seven fifty-five."

"And when did you come home?"

"I don't know. Uh...maybe eight fifteen."

"And when you got home, she was lying on the patio?"

"Yes."

"Was she conscious?"

"No."

"Breathing?"

His hand goes to his cheek, and he gets a confused look on his face. "I...I don't know. I couldn't tell."

A man comes to the doorframe and makes eye contact with the woman.

"James, I need you to come with me," she says, and James turns to look at the man in the doorframe. Carol comes forward and takes James by the hand. James stands, stumbles, then follows her to the front room where she has him sit on the couch.

"Is my wife alive?"

"Yes. But she's not in good condition. We're taking her to EIRMC."

"The hospital?"

"Yes."

The sound of a stretcher wheeling down the hall brings his head around. They watch as the injured woman is taken out the front door.

"James, would you like to go in the ambulance?"

"Yes, please."

Chapter 5

Hank and Joyce

Hank pulls the car to the curb of the address Joyce was given and whistles. Joyce says nothing, gazing at the home. Two police vehicles are out front, and caution tape surrounds the property. Several neighbors watch as Joyce and Hank exit the vehicle and walk down the driveway. At the bottom of the stairs, leading to the front door, Officer O'Malley stands waiting for them. She nods as they approach.

"Detectives."

"How are you, Carol?" Joyce asks.

O'Malley turns and leads them up the stairs toward the entrance.

"Sad situation here."

"What happened?"

They enter the house, and Hank looks around, marveling at the size. Joyce keeps her eyes trained on Officer O'Malley.

"A mother of four fell off the balcony near the bedroom. She landed on the back patio."

They walk down the hall. The forensic team seems to be everywhere. The two women walk through the kitchen as Hank falls behind. Joyce turns to look for him, and he sees it and quickens his pace. O'Malley guides them out the back door to the patio. An outline of where the body landed, along with a smattering of blood and body fluids, cover the area.

"Did anyone see her fall?" Joyce asks, looking up at the balcony.

O'Malley shakes her head. "The husband came home and found her."

"She was alone?"

A broken laptop sits in the grass, and O'Malley points to it. "She was logging in to a Zoom meeting when she walked out and fell. At least, that's what we've gathered."

"She works from home?"

"No, she has an office in town, but apparently works out on the balcony from time to time."

"What does she do?"

"CEO of a clothing brand. Started a few years ago. Judging by the place, she's doing well."

Joyce nods. "Show us to the balcony?"

O'Malley goes in front, and they walk behind her, climbing the staircase and entering through the double doors of the master suite. The room is larger than any bedroom Hank has ever seen. On the backside of the room, a set of doors leads out to the balcony. The doors are open. They survey the room, then walk to the balcony and stop at the threshold.

On the balcony is a small table and two chairs. It's the railing that holds Joyce's attention. It looks too low.

"Am I okay to step out there?" she asks O'Malley.

"Yes, forensics is done here."

She nods and steps onto the balcony. As she does, she begins to slip, and Hank reaches out and grabs her. They frown at each other and look down at the surface. The balcony is made of composite wood and shouldn't be that slippery. Joyce bends down and runs a finger along the floor. She smells it, then gets on all fours and sniffs the ground. A frown darkens her complexion. She stands, hands on hips, surveying the area around the house. She looks at the railing surrounding the balcony.

"Do either of you know what code is for the height of a railing?"

O'Malley shakes her head, but Hank says, "Thirty-six inches, I believe."

Joyce nods and asks O'Malley to fetch her a tape measure. Joyce and Hank look at each other, an unspoken message passing between them. O'Malley returns and hands Joyce the tool she requested. Joyce measures the railing, and it only reaches twenty-eight inches. She looks at the furniture. The small table sits in the middle of the balcony, the two chairs on the side. Joyce goes over and sits in the chair closest to the table. She mimes placing a laptop on the table and typing. Her body is at an angle.

"How tall is Mrs. Burch?"

O'Malley looks through her notes. "Five feet two inches."

"Hmm," she says and stands. She walks carefully to the railing and looks down at the patio, then turns back. "Officer, this is a crime scene. Make sure you note in your report this was no accident. Someone pushed her from the balcony."

Chapter 6

Rita

"Mr. Burch?"

A woman with long, black hair pulled back in a ponytail stands looking down at James. She has large, dark eyes and lovely, long eyelashes. She's wearing medical scrubs, white sneakers, and a white coat. Her name and title are embroidered on the left side of the coat. James sits alone in a family waiting room, staring at the floor. With the mention of his name, his head comes up. His eyes look lost.

I'm the injured woman. The lifeless body lying on a bed in a room down the hall is mine. After the ambulance reached the hospital, the emergency response team rushed my body inside the emergency wing. Curious, I followed, leaving James as he went through the main entrance.

They took my body up the elevator, down the hall, and into a large room. Multiple doctors and nurses went to work, stabbing my arm with a needle and inserting an IV, running scans and many tests, including X-rays. They hooked me up to machines, including a ventilator. Because I have no physical shape in this state, I watched everyone work simultaneously, no matter where they stood in the room. I realized my perspective wasn't limited to where my attention focused. I could see everything all at once.

After two hours, the doctor left my bedside, cleaned herself up, and went in search of James. That's when I recognized my ability to change location. As she searched for him, I merely thought about him and found myself transported to his side.

"Yes, I'm James Burch."

"Hello, James. My name is Dr. Mitchell. I've been assigned as the lead doctor for your wife, Rita. Will you come with me, please?"

James follows her to a small consultation room down the hall. She opens the door, and James enters. She holds the door open as a new man in a white coat joins her.

"James, this is my colleague, Dr. Habib."

James walks from the doorframe and extends his hand to Dr. Habib. Dr. Habib is a small man with large glasses and curly black hair that's graying. Dr. Mitchell sits in the chair across from James while Dr. Habib pulls a chair from against the wall.

"James, we wanted to talk to you. I'm sure you're eager to know how your wife is doing."

James wipes his hands on the sweatpants he's been wearing since he found my body. He nods anxiously.

"There's no easy way to say this. Your wife is badly hurt. She has multiple fractures, including her spine, her hand, both of her legs, and her pelvis. She also has a fracture in her skull, which has caused a subdural hematoma. Are you familiar with what that is?"

James shakes his head.

Dr. Mitchell holds up her hand and separates her thumb from her index finger. "There's a space between the brain and skull connected by veins. Some of those veins broke because of the force with which your wife hit the patio. That has caused bleeding, resulting in damage to your wife's brain. At this point, we don't know how extensive that damage is."

The doctor stops and pauses, seeing James's face drain of color. She passes a box of tissues across the table, and he takes one, dabbing at his eyes.

"Is my wife still alive?"

Dr. Mitchell looks at Dr. Habib, then back at James. She places a hand on the table. "Her heart is still beating, and she's breathing, although she's been placed on a ventilator. She was unconscious when she arrived, and her heart stopped. We had to resuscitate her. It was shaky, but she came back. We've sedated her; although I don't think she'd wake, anyway. She's in a coma. For now, we're still working to determine just how significant her injuries are. We'll learn a lot more in the next twenty-four hours."

"So, she's alive?"

Dr. Mitchell looks at Dr. Habib.

"Technically, yes," Dr. Habib says. "However, if we took her off the machines, she wouldn't be able to breathe on her own. There seems to be very little brain function."

I can't believe what I'm hearing. How could this be? My brain is working. I'm here watching them. Conscious of everything.

James frowns. "What does that mean?"

Dr. Mitchell responds. "It means that your wife's brain isn't giving commands to the rest of her body."

Is that right? Maybe I just haven't tried.

"She's a vegetable?"

"I wouldn't say that. It's too early to tell. It might just be a shock. Her brain might bounce back. It's too early to know for sure."

James looks at them and nods. "Okay. Can I see her?"

"Certainly."

Dr. Mitchell stands and opens the door while James and Dr. Habib follow her. She guides them down the hall and stops in front of the closed door. She turns back to James.

"She's not conscious, and she won't be able to respond, but you can talk to her."

How does she know that? I haven't even tried. Maybe that's all it will take.

James nods, and Dr. Mitchell opens the door.

My body lays in the bed connected to a seemingly endless number of machines. A bank of monitors line the wall beside me. My clothes were removed, and I'm wearing a hospital gown. The hair on my head has been cut short, and there's swelling around the face and eyes. I have no memory of what I looked like before, but I imagine it was quite different.

"You can go close to her, touch her. Just stay clear of any equipment."

James steps to the bed with trepidation. He reaches a trembling hand toward me but stops.

"You can touch her," Dr. Mitchell says.

He looks back at her but doesn't. He moves closer to my head and looks at my face.

Why won't he touch me?

"You can talk to her," Dr. Mitchell encourages.

James turns and sees both doctors watching him. A woman in a slightly different outfit entered while his back was turned. She walks over and writes her name on the whiteboard on the far wall. She's a short woman with big, green eyes and long, auburn hair.

"My name is Ginger," she says, waving. "I'll be here taking care of Rita."

James nods and turns back to me. "Rita? It's your husband, James."

I don't respond, but for the first time since the accident, I feel a connection to my body, a longing to go back. I try to enter it, but something is preventing me. It's as if a force field blocks me from my physical form.

"I'm going to stay here with you. Please fight and come back."

His words sound hollow. Forced. As if he's acting for the doctors. Doesn't he want me to come back? The doctors look at each other, and Dr. Mitchell steps to him, putting a hand on his shoulder.

"James, we're going to leave you for a while. We'll be monitoring her progress. Please let the nurse know if you need anything."

James nods, and the doctors slip out of the room. The door closes, then opens again. A woman stands in the doorframe. She's wearing black leggings, a bright blue top, and matching blue sneakers.

"James?" she says, and the nurse and James turn in her direction. She has blonde hair and bright blue eyes. She's wearing lipstick and has long fake eyelashes. Her clothes are tight, and I highly doubt her breasts are real. She rushes forward and puts a hand on James's shoulder.

The nurse comes forward. "Ma'am, you can't be in here. Only family."

The new woman turns on her, annoyance in her eyes. James sees the two women looking at each other and stands. "It's okay. Kim is our neighbor. I asked her to come."

Kim gives a look to the nurse like, "I told you so." Then turns back to James. She rubs his arm, looking up into his eyes. "I'm so sorry." She reaches out for him, and he steps to her.

Ginger, the nurse, is undeterred. "I understand, but she still can't be here. You're welcome to go out to the waiting room to talk."

James nods, and Kim scowls at Ginger. Ginger returns her look with a smile, and James moves toward the door. Kim follows. When they're out in the hall, Kim puts a hand on James's back and rubs it as they walk, her eyes looking up at him. "Are you okay? What happened?"

James walks along in a daze. They reach the waiting room of the intensive care unit and enter. An elderly woman sits at the far end of the room. James and Kim select seats near the door. James sits first, and Kim sits next to him, her knee touching his leg.

Who is this woman? I don't remember her. Why is she touching him like this?

"James? What happened?"

James shakes his head. "I don't know. I came home, and Rita was on the patio, unconscious."

"How?"

"I don't know. I called 9-1-1, and you saw her, she's not doing good."

James holds one hand, palm up, and picks at it with the other. Kim rubs his shoulder.

I don't like her touching my husband. What's going on between them?

"Is she going to make it?"

He shakes his head. "I don't know."

"Oh, I'm so sorry. What can I do for you? Do you need me to take the kids?"

James looks at her, then at the clock on the wall. "I'm supposed to drive carpool today for the younger ones."

Kim shakes her head. "Don't worry about that. I'll get them."

James nods. "Thank you. The older boys, David and Donovan, can drive themselves. They should be home in about an hour."

"Do you want me to go over? Talk to them?"

The door to the waiting room opens, and a large black man steps inside, followed by a small white woman in her mid fifties. The man wears a dark blue suit with a matching blue tie and a white shirt. The woman is in a dark green pantsuit. James and Kim look up and watch them cross the room and sit on a couch. Neither speaks. They sit together, but they aren't a couple. There's a familiarity between them, but it's not sexual.

Kim turns back to James, her hand resting on his. "James, do you want me to tell them about Rita?"

James hesitates. "No, I want to tell them. Can you bring them here? Wait for the younger two, then bring them all."

"Sure," Kim says and reaches forward and hugs him. She stands. "I'll be back in a few minutes. Hang in there. It's going to be okay."

James nods, but his look is hollow. He's not hearing her anymore.

Maybe I'm wrong about her. Maybe she's only being nice. He has been through a lot and doesn't seem to be functioning on all cylinders.

When the door shuts and Kim is gone, the newcomers stand and each pulls something from their pockets.

"Mr. Burch?" the woman says. "My name is Detective Joyce Powers, and this is Hank Gardener. We're with the Idaho Falls Police Department. We've been assigned to investigate your wife's accident. Can we talk to you for a few minutes?"

Chapter 7

I watch as James looks up at the two people standing before him.

"Detectives?"

"Yes," Joyce says. "Do you mind if we sit for a few minutes?"

Hank doesn't wait for an answer and pulls a seat around for Joyce, then one for himself. They sit side by side on chairs in front of James while he remains on the couch. James looks at the family sitting at the other end of the room. Joyce turns to look at them, then back to James.

"Don't worry. They're too far away to hear us. We'll keep our voices low."

James shakes his head. "I don't understand. Why would you be investigating what happened to Rita? It was an accident."

"Was it?" Hank asks, looking at James, his face impassive.

James looks confused. "Huh?"

Joyce keeps her voice low and looks at him with sympathetic eyes. "It's our job to find out if it truly was an accident. It certainly might have been, but on the off chance it wasn't, we need to know. Your assistance in answering some of our questions would be very helpful."

James looks from her to Hank and back again. "Okay."

"Good. Can you tell us about what happened this morning?"

"I don't know what happened. I came home, and she was on the patio, unconscious."

Joyce nods. "Right, but before that. Take us through the morning."

James leans forward and puts his hand to his forehead, looking down. "Rita went to the gym early."

"About what time?" Hank asks.

James sits up and looks at him. "She goes to a workout class at five thirty every morning. It lasts for an hour. My alarm goes off at six fifteen, but I must have hit snooze because I don't remember it."

"You don't remember it going off?" Hank asks.

"Uh...not really. And next thing I know, the doorbell rings, then an announcement that someone was at the front door."

"An announcement?" Hank asks.

"Yes, we have a speaker system that alerts us if someone is at the front door."

"Is that on all the doors? Or just the front door?"

"The front door and walkout basement."

"Okay, go on."

Hank has a notepad out and is taking notes. Joyce sits back in her chair, listening.

"Anyway, I looked at my phone, and it said six forty-eight. I remember the time because I wondered who could be at the door that early."

"Was the alarm on your phone? Or did you have an alarm clock?"

"My phone. I use a sleep app."

"Got it."

He pauses and seems to fight for his thoughts. "Anyway, I climbed out of bed and walked down the stairs. It was Rita at the door."

"Was that normal for Rita to come home and come to the front door?"

"No."

"How does she normally come through the house?"

"The garage."

"She parks her car in the garage?"

"Yes."

"Okay, please go on."

James talks to Joyce now. "So, I let her in, and she was mad."

"At you?" Hank asks.

"Yes."

"Why?"

"Because I didn't get the boys up, and they were going to be late for school."

Hank makes a note in his notepad and then waves for James to go on.

"After she yelled at me, she went downstairs, and I went upstairs. I got the younger boys up while she worked on the older ones. Eventually, we all met in the kitchen. Well...not David. He was too late and ate nothing, just went straight to the car and Donovan followed. I had to get the younger boys to middle school. I drove the carpool and left."

Why can't I remember any of this? It's so frustrating.

"You say your wife yelled at you?"

James shakes his head. "Not yelled. She was angry. Frustrated."

"Does that happen a lot? Rita getting angry with you? And do you get angry with her?"

James pauses and looks at them individually. "No."

Joyce has been a silent bystander. She hasn't asked a question or made a sound. Now, Hank follows suit. Neither of them speaks, and James squirms in his chair.

"What?" James asks.

"Have you ever raised a hand to your wife?"

James looks at him sharply. "What?"

"Nothing," Hank says, shaking his head. "Where was Rita?"

James stares at him for a bit. "When?"

"When you left the house to run the carpool."

"She watched us go."

"From the garage?"

"Yes."

"You didn't talk to her before you left?"

James looks at Hank, then shakes his head.

"Your last words to each other were when she yelled at you?"

"She didn't yell. I misspoke when I said that."

Hank narrows his eyes on him. "Okay. When she was frustrated with you?"

"Yes."

"How many kids are in the carpool?"

"Two."

"Just your kids?"

"No, besides my kids."

"So, you picked them up, dropped them at school, then came home?"

"Right."

"You didn't go anywhere else?"

"No."

"Did anyone see you?"

"Besides the kids in the carpool?"

"Yes."

"I don't know. Maybe."

"Like whom?"

"I don't know, maybe neighbors. I don't remember."

"Okay, so you got home...and how did you enter?"

"I parked in the garage."

"Then where'd you go?"

"The kitchen."

"What did you do?"

"Got some coffee and went to find Rita."

"Why?"

"Because I wanted to talk to her. I don't like something between us."

"Were you angry? Maybe wanted to teach her a lesson?"

"Huh?"

"You heard me."

James's tone becomes hard. "I would never hurt Rita. *Never.*"

Hank nods. "Okay. When did you see her?"

James looks up at the ceiling, avoiding their eyes. "After getting the coffee, I went upstairs. I planned to apologize for not getting up. But I knew she'd probably be on a call, so I planned to just hang out in our room and wait. But when I went into our room, I didn't hear her. I noticed she'd left her coffee cup on the nightstand, and the balcony doors were open."

"That was unusual?"

"Sort of. Why would someone get coffee and then leave it on the nightstand?"

"What about the balcony doors being open? Was that common?"

"Yes. Rita likes to work out there when the weather's nice."

"So, then what?"

"I didn't see her on the balcony. So, I went and looked."

James sits forward and puts his head in his hands. He begins to tremble, and Hank looks at Joyce. Joyce gets James a box of tissues and hands it to him. After a moment, James controls himself and looks up.

"Sorry," James says.

"It's okay. We understand," Joyce says. "James, just a couple more questions, and we'll let you get back to Rita."

He nods.

"Did you notice anything unusual this morning? Anything out of the ordinary?"

James scoffs. "Other than my wife dead on the patio?"

Joyce just watches him.

"No."

"Nothing?"

James shakes his head. "I don't know. I don't remember my phone alarm going off. Actually, it wasn't in sleep mode when I picked it up."

Hank makes a note and Joyce nods.

"What about the balcony? Anything unusual there?" Joyce asks.

James shakes his head.

"Do you ever iron clothes?"

"What?"

"Clothes. Do you ever iron clothes? Maybe spray your collared shirts with starch?"

"No."

"Does Rita?"

"No. I do the laundry most of the time now."

"Oh? And you never iron?"

"I don't know, maybe occasionally."

"Where do you do it when you iron?"

"Downstairs, near the laundry room."

"Never upstairs, maybe in your room?"

"No."

Joyce nods. "What were you saying about your wife?"

"Huh?"

"Your wife, you were saying something about her before I interrupted."

He squints as he tries to remember. "Oh. Rita is the CEO of BEAU, the clothing brand. She works, and I stay home with the kids. I'm a stay-at-home dad."

Joyce nods. "For how long?"

James shrugs. "About two years. Rita started BEAU three years ago. It took off. She was making a lot more money than me, so we decided I should stay at home with the kids."

The door opens, and Ginger, the nurse, stands in the doorway with a large teenage boy.

"Dad?"

Chapter 8

The large teenage boy with wavy brown hair and dark-brown eyes pushes past the nurse.

"Dad, what's going on? What happened to Rita?"

Why is my son calling me by my name?

James stands from the couch as more teenage boys file into the room, followed by Kim, the neighbor. She's changed her outfit. She's wearing a sundress with a plunging neckline. The oldest and largest boy stands nose to nose with his father.

"There was an accident."

"What kind of accident?" the boy demands.

James looks past him to the other boys. Kim raises her palms and mouths, "I'm sorry" to James. The second oldest stands behind his bigger brother. He's a few inches shorter and twenty pounds lighter. The oldest looks angry, while the younger looks frightened. The youngest two stand by Kim. The smallest has tears in his eyes.

Are all of these boys my sons?

"Come here," James says, leading the boys to the couch. "Let's talk."

The three youngest come forward and sit on the couch, but the oldest doesn't move, glaring at his father. Kim remains by the door while Hank and Joyce, seeing the family needs space, stand and cross the room but remain close enough to listen and watch.

James pulls the chair Hank was sitting in and puts it next to the couch, then turns to his oldest son. "David, please, have a seat."

David finally relents and sits down, crossing his arms. James pulls the chair Joyce was using and sits before his boys.

"Your mom had an accident," James says.

The lip of the youngest trembles, and the second son looks at him, then back to his father.

"What kind of accident?" David asks.

"After I came home from driving the carpool, I found her on the patio behind the house." James looks at the detectives, then back at the boys. The boys glance over at them as well. "She was unconscious. We think she fell off the balcony from our room."

"Fell? How? Is she dead?" David says.

James holds up a hand. "No, no. But it's serious. She's in a coma. She has several broken bones, and the doctors are doing a lot of tests on her."

Now the second youngest starts to cry. He stands and throws his arms around his father. The youngest joins him, and James sits holding our two youngest sons while seated in the chair. The second oldest remains on the couch, a shell-shocked look on his face. It's harder to see because of his glasses, but his eyes appear red. David, the oldest, looks down. After a couple of minutes, the boys release their father and retake their place on the couch. James rubs his cheeks and takes some deep breaths.

"Would you like to see her?"

The youngest two look at their oldest brother, and when he nods, they follow. The second son doesn't reply, looking at his hands.

"Okay. Let me go check with the nurse."

James stands and looks at Kim, and she nods. She steps aside as James exits.

Kim walks over to stand in front of the boys. "I was going to go down to the cafeteria. Do you guys want me to bring you anything? Soda? Maybe some cookies?"

The youngest two nod, asking for root beer and orange soda. The third son doesn't look at her, and the oldest shrugs and asks for "ice cream or something." The youngest two like that idea and ask for that as well. Kim smiles and turns for the door when it opens, and James comes back into the room. She touches his arm and looks up at him.

"Would you like anything?"

"Maybe just some water."

"Sure." She smiles and leaves.

She really is very sweet. Maybe I was wrong about something going on between them.

James faces our boys. "Guys, I can only take you one at a time, and you can't stay for long. Who wants to go first?"

None of the boys volunteer and, eventually, David stands. James puts an arm around his shoulder, and they walk out. I follow as they head down the hall. When David reaches the room, he stops and lets

James go first. James waves him in and David enters. His eyes go wide when he sees my body and the machines surrounding it.

"You can talk to her," James tells him. "The doctors think it might help."

David stands motionless, staring at me.

After several seconds, James asks, "Do you want to say anything to her?"

David looks at James, but he doesn't reply. He swallows and then speaks in a hushed tone.

"I'm sorry this happened to you."

"You can touch her. If you want."

"I don't want to," he says and turns around and walks out of the room.

James rushes to catch up and puts an arm around him. They walk down the hall without speaking. When they enter the waiting room, David sits in the same chair without looking up.

He seems angry. Is he angry with me or because of what happened to me?

"Donovan? Do you want to go next?" James asks.

Donovan sits looking at the ground. He shakes his head.

James turns to the next son. "Gilbert?"

Gilbert stands, looks at Donovan, then seeing no reaction from him turns back to his father. James puts his arm around him and walks him down. When Gilbert enters the room, he moves closer to the bed but hesitates.

"It's okay," James tells him. "You can touch her. Just be gentle."

Gilbert tentatively reaches out but stops before touching me. I'm not sure how it works, because I don't have my body, but I feel it. It's not a touch per se, more like an electric impulse as his hand gets close.

"Sorry, Mom."

The force of the electricity is even stronger. He looks frightened, and James puts an arm around him and takes him out.

As they walk down the hall, Gilbert asks, "Is she going to be okay?"

"I don't know, buddy. I wish I did."

They enter the room, and Gilbert takes his place on the couch.

James looks at the youngest. "Reed, do you want to go?"

Reed stands, and James does the same with him, wrapping an arm around his shoulders. When Reed enters the room, he looks at me, then up at his dad.

"You can talk to her and even touch her, just be gentle."

James steps close to me but doesn't touch. Reed steps closer, but he doesn't reach out. Even the movement of his body close to mine does something to me. I feel it. My connection to him is so strong.

He looks at my face, and I so badly want to open my eyes for him, to soothe his hurt.

"Get better, Mom."

The silence in the room is deafening. After several seconds, they leave, and I go with them down the hall. When we enter the waiting room, I notice Hank and Joyce are gone. The boys are alone, and the other family on the other side has left as well. Reed sits on the couch, and Kim reenters the room. She's carrying a soda tray and has cookies. She passes them out to the boys. They all take them, except Donovan. She offers a cookie, but he waves her away.

"Donovan? Do you want to go see your mom?" James asks.

He looks up at his dad and shakes his head, then looks back down. James nods. Kim offers James a cookie, and he takes it, thanking her.

"Is there anything you need from home?" Kim asks.

"I'm not sure. I'll let you know."

"Do you want me to take the boys?"

James nods, and the youngest two complain.

"You can come back tomorrow," James tells them.

Donovan stands from the couch and walks out of the room. James follows. Donovan is walking away from my room when James calls out to him. "Hey, buddy. She's over here."

When Donovan turns around, tears stream down his face. "I don't want to see her, okay?"

The nurses at the station turn and look at him. Every eye in the ICU watches their interaction. Donovan looks away and sees everyone staring at him. He turns and runs. Donovan reaches the doors and pushes through them, knocking over a woman. James runs after him. Donovan stops and extends his hand to the woman but sees James coming toward him. He pulls back his hand and bolts for the stairs.

Chapter 9

After Donovan ran out of the hospital, James returned and got the other boys, saying he couldn't find him. He asked Kim to give them all a ride home since James didn't have his car. Now I'm alone for the first time since seeing my body on the patio behind our house. My consciousness moves down the hall, past the nurses' station, and into my hospital room.

I look at my body, my chest rising and falling with the ventilator, and wonder who I am. I know my name, Rita Burch. I know James is my husband, and we have four sons, although I wonder why the oldest calls me by my name rather than mom. Maybe James was married before. Maybe David isn't really my son. The thought brings a wave of frustration. Why can't I remember? I remember nothing about myself or anyone else. It's as if the fall from the balcony erased my entire life.

I think back to the conversation James had with the doctors. I could tell from their somber expressions and hushed tones that things weren't looking good. I knew that from the accident and my initial hours after arriving at the hospital. But hearing it from the doctors made it more real. They don't think I'll wake.

A different nurse, not Ginger, enters the room. She fiddles with one machine, changes the IV bag hanging above my head, looks me over, and exits. I take a moment to look at myself more closely. My eyes are closed, and my body is still, other than the rise and fall of my chest. I look like I could be dead. My skin is pale, almost blue. I wonder if it's cold. My lips are full but gray. My hair is short and buzzed. There's bruising and swelling around my forehead. My cheekbones are high, and my eyelashes are long. Mascara covers them. I have crow's feet.

I look more closely at my body. I'm relatively thin, maybe 130 pounds. I can't tell how tall I am, but I don't think I could be taller than five-three. A scar runs along my right hand, and I rack my brain, trying to remember how I got it. I force myself to focus, but it's blank. It's as if the memory never existed. My frustration boils over, and if I could, I'd kick and punch my arms and legs. Instead, they lie lifeless on the bed.

The only memories I have are from the time right after I fell until now. That reminds me, detectives were here. Why? What did they hope to find? Was it really like they told James? Are they checking boxes? Or do they think something else happened? Do they think someone hurt me? Or maybe I hurt myself? Maybe James? My mind focuses on the female detective. The woman with the kind eyes. I force myself to concentrate on her. Suddenly, she sits before me. She's on a couch next to a man about her age. They're watching a movie. He's immersed in it, hand in a bowl of popcorn, a smile on his face. His eyes move as he watches the action.

She has a hand on his thigh, the other between her knees. She leans a shoulder on him. She's turned toward the screen, but she's somewhere else. Her eyes aren't moving to follow the action. Her eyes remain forward, unblinking. It's as if the screen is blank. A small dog lies on the couch beside her. I look around the room and then out the window. It's night, but the sun hasn't completely dropped behind the mountains to the west.

How is this possible? My mind goes back to the hospital room and my body lying on the bed. As quickly as I think about it, I'm there, seeing my body again. I look out the window and see the sun is in the same position. I wonder if this works with other people too. I focus my mind on Hank, the other detective. Just like with Joyce, I see him before me. He's out at dinner. A pretty woman sits beside him. They appear to be on a date. Another couple is on the other side of the booth. A bowl of chips and salsa sits on the table, and they all have drinks. Hank is telling a story, and they're hanging on his every word. He's animated, waving his hands and laughing.

Next, I think about Donovan. He sits on a lounge chair, his feet propped up. He holds a video game controller and watches the screen. He's playing some type of first-person shooter game and periodically moves as if he's part of it. His anger seems to have subsided. He's in his element now. Is it an escape?

My consciousness floats around the house. All the boys are home, except David. Reed is outside shooting baskets on the full court we have behind the house. Gilbert is on the main floor in the family room watching YouTube on the TV. My consciousness goes upstairs to our bedroom. I check the balcony and the bathroom. He's nowhere. I float to the other rooms. Not there either.

I get an idea and check the garage. Three cars are there. A white Mercedes Benz S Class, a silver Chevrolet Tahoe, and a blue Ford F-150. I look inside each car but don't see James. I'm about to leave the area when movement catches my eye. James is up on a ladder. He's adjusting something on one of the two overhead garage door openers. A remote is in his hand. Why would he spend his time doing this? His wife lays unconscious in a hospital bed fighting for her life, and he's fiddling with the garage doors. Something isn't right.

Chapter 10

Ethan

Ethan Stone pulls his white, ten-year-old Honda Civic to the curb behind the KIDK 3 news van, cuts the lights, and shuts off the engine. He exits the car, slamming the door, and stalks to the driver's side of the van, glancing at the small group of people standing on the other side of the street. Colby, the cameraman, sits behind the wheel reading a Wikipedia page on his phone. Seeing Ethan standing outside the window, he sleeps the phone and pulls open the door but doesn't exit.

"About time you got here. They've wanted to cut to us twice already."

"It's not my fault. I'm off today, remember?" Ethan snarls. "I was at dinner with Julie when I got the call. First time I've had a full day off in eleven days, and now it's ruined. What is this, anyway?"

Colby points to the house across the street. "The woman in that house fell from her back balcony. She's in intensive care."

Ethan frowns. "So?"

"So," Colby says, standing from the seat and shutting the van door, "she's the owner of a huge clothing brand." He walks to the back of the van and opens the door, pulling out a camera. "Ever heard of BEAU?"

"No."

"You better read this then." He unlocks his phone and thrusts it at Ethan. Ethan takes it as Colby fiddles with the camera, then hands him a mic and earpiece. Ethan puts the earpiece in his ear while still holding the phone, reading the station director's note.

"Wow," Ethan says. "And she lived here?"

"Yep."

"So, what kind of shot are we doing? Something simple in front of the house?"

Colby shoulders the camera and motions to the group of people standing around, watching them. "One neighbor says she was friends with Rita Burch. She's willing to be interviewed on air." Colby motions to a lean woman with blonde hair, and she steps away from the group and comes toward them. "Ethan, this is Kim Long. Kim, Ethan."

Ethan extends his hand to her. "Nice to meet you, Kim." She smiles and takes his hand. "You know Mrs. Burch well?"

"Yes, we were friends."

He smiles and presses his finger to his ear, listening to instructions from the news director. Kim watches him while Colby sets up his camera and turns on a bright light. Colby motions to Ethan, and Ethan steps in front of the camera. Kim walks to him.

"Kim, why don't you stand right here? This is going to be a live shot, so I'm going to talk for a few seconds, then walk over to you. I'll ask you a few questions about Rita and your relationship with her. Just be yourself and talk to me. Don't worry about the camera. Pretend we're just having a conversation, okay?"

She nods.

"Have you ever been on TV before?"

She rocks back and forth. "Once or twice."

He smiles. "Oh, good. Then you're a pro. Focus on me, not the camera."

He steps away from her and moves back to stand in front of Colby and the camera. The Burch house is behind him. Ethan straightens his shoulders and looks into the camera. After a few seconds, he gets a solemn look on his face.

"That's right, Nancy. I'm here outside the scene of Rita Burch's tragic accident. I've been speaking with some neighbors, and this sudden tragedy shocks them." He turns and motions to the house. "Rita Burch, founder and CEO of BEAU, a huge clothing label, was found unresponsive after having fallen from her patio behind this house. As you can see, the height was extreme, and she currently lies in a hospital bed fighting for her life." He drops his hand and straightens his shoulders to the camera. "We've been talking to the neighbors and have Kim Long, her close friend and neighbor, here with us." He takes a few steps as Colby swings his camera to see both of them. "Kim, thanks for joining us tonight. How is everyone holding up after this tragedy?"

Kim shakes her head. "We're shocked. Rita is so admired by everyone in the neighborhood, and we feel so much for her family."

Ethan nods, his face grave. "I understand you were close to Mrs. Burch."

"Yes, that's correct. I worked out with her every day, and we became close friends, not just neighbors."

"What can you tell us about Rita?"

Kim folds her arms in front of her. "She was so smart. She created the BEAU label all by herself. She did that while caring for her husband and four sons. Everything she accomplished amazed everyone."

Ethan shakes his head. "Tragic. Have you heard anything about how she's doing?"

Kim nods. "Actually, I was there at the hospital with the family today."

"You were?"

"Yes."

"How are they doing?"

"They're shocked. Very upset, as you can imagine."

"Did you learn anything about her prognosis?"

Kim tears up while looking at the camera. "She's in a coma and not doing good. It's unlikely that she'll live through this."

"Is that what the doctors said?"

Realizing she's staring at the camera, she quickly turns back to Ethan, wipes her eyes, and nods. "I heard it from her husband."

Ethan gets a somber look on his face and nods. "Thank you, Kim, for taking the time to talk to us tonight. I'm sure you're such a boon to the family."

Chapter 11

Rita

Joyce climbs into the Dodge Charger and smiles at Hank as he sits behind the wheel. "Good morning," Hank says, handing her a cup of coffee, two creams, and one sugar.

Last night, after my family went to bed and David came home, I went back to the hospital. I watched my body in the bed, occasionally being checked by doctors and nurses. I wondered how I might learn about myself and decided my best course was to follow the detectives investigating my accident. I want to know if someone tried to kill me. The hours dragged as I waited for morning.

"Thank you," Joyce says.

Hank puts the car in drive, and they pull away from the police station.

"Big day today," Joyce says, sipping on the coffee.

Hank looks over and nods. "Any new thoughts since yesterday?"

Joyce shrugs and looks out the window. "Lots. I haven't been able to think of anything else. What about you?"

"Same."

"Sam wasn't happy about it last night."

"Oh?"

"Yeah, I guess he wanted me to be *present*." Joyce shakes her head. "I'm not sure why it matters. I was sitting with him while we watched his action movie. It's not like we ever discuss it. What's there to discuss anyway? It's a bunch of fake explosions and tough guys walking around pretending to be intelligent. Can I help it if it doesn't interest me like it does him?"

Hank takes his eyes off the road and glances at her.

"What? You like them?" she says.

Hank shrugs. "Depends."

She waves a hand. "It's fine. When you've been married for thirty years, it happens." Joyce turns in her seat and focuses her eyes on him. "Speaking of, when are you going to make an honest woman out of Saundra?"

Hank laughs. "Honest woman?"

"It's just an expression," Joyce says and takes a sip of her coffee while keeping her eyes on him. He shoots a glance at her but keeps focused on driving.

"I've tried. A better question for her."

Joyce stares at him, expressionless.

"What?"

Joyce turns back to the window.

"So, you had a lot of thoughts, any you want to share?"

"Interesting family."

"Yeah. Do you think it was the husband?"

Joyce pauses. "How many homicides have you worked?"

"Here? Or total?"

Joyce smiles at him. "Is the number different?"

He chuckles, turning the wheel. "No."

Joyce tips her shoulder and turns back to the window.

"One," Hank says.

"And who did it?"

Hank sighs. Joyce knows the answer. They worked it together. "The husband."

"I've worked about twenty over my career. In every case, the victim knew the killer. Nine out of ten, the killer was the person closest to the victim."

"So, you think it was James?"

"I think we have to start there. He likely has the most to gain, and he's the one who found her."

"But?"

She turns away from the window and looks at him. "But this one's different."

"How so?"

"That's the same question I kept asking myself last night. It's a homicide, I'm sure of it. Well...at least an attempted homicide. But every one of those other murders was a crime of passion. This wasn't. This one was cold and calculated. And it's like I always tell you, we have to figure out who had opportunity and motive. Today will go a long way in helping us answer those questions."

"So, you don't think it's him?"

"I didn't say that. I just said this one's different."

So, he planned it? Is that what she's saying? Maybe he worked with someone else?

They pull into the parking lot, park, exit the vehicle, and walk inside the glass doors to the building. A striking blonde woman with long hair who seems to glow sits behind the desk. She's young, maybe mid twenties. She holds a phone to her ear and smiles at them while holding up a finger.

"Erin," she says into the phone. "Mark is on the line. He wants to talk to you." The woman replaces the receiver and looks up at the detectives. "Can I help you?"

Joyce and Hank hold out their badges, but Hank speaks. "Yes, we're detectives with the Idaho Falls Police Department. We need to speak with whoever's in charge."

The girl frowns. "Well, that would be Rita. But she's not in."

Hank nods. "Okay, in that case, who would be next in line after Mrs. Burch?"

The girl puts her finger to her lips. "Let me get you Erin."

"Thank you."

"You can have a seat over there. Her line's busy. I'll let her know when she's off."

Hank and Joyce walk to the small waiting area below the stairs. Hank takes the loveseat, and Joyce opts for the chair. They don't speak while looking around the office. The building is new, with marble floors and floor-to-ceiling glass walls and doors. Nobody appears to be on the main floor of the two-story building, aside from the receptionist. The visible offices have For Lease signs adorning the walls. It seems most of the building is vacant.

After a few minutes, the receptionist rings Erin and then comes over to them. She wears a tight white dress with tall heels. Her dress is short, revealing her shapely legs.

"She'll be right down."

A woman descends the stairs. She's older than the receptionist, but no less beautiful. She has light-brown hair that falls across her shoulders. She's tall, at least five-ten, and her heels put her over six feet.

"Hello," she says after reaching the bottom and walking toward them. She extends a hand as Hank and Joyce stand. She reaches out to Joyce first, towering over her. Next, she smiles at Hank and extends her hand to him. "I'm Erin, Rita's assistant. Will you join me in the conference room?"

She turns and leads them up the stairs to a room they could see from the lower level. The space features a large boardroom table and a whiteboard on the wall. Ten leather swivel chairs surround the table. A large *B* is emblazoned into the wood in the center. Erin motions for them to sit, and they take chairs beside one another, sinking into the plush seats. Erin glides around the table and sits across from them. She's seated on the edge of the chair, her posture impeccable. Her back doesn't touch the rest behind her. She folds one hand over the other, resting them on the boardroom table.

"Are you here about Rita?"

"We are," Hank replies. "We're looking into what happened to her."

Erin puts her hand to her cheek and sighs. She has long, lovely red nails that complement her slender hand. They match her blouse and lipstick. She looks like she belongs in a fashion magazine. "James called last night and told me what happened. I cried. I couldn't believe it. I kept calling all day and couldn't reach her. Now I know why." She pauses and looks at them more closely. "James said it was an accident. Why are you looking into it?"

Hank waves a hand. "Standard procedure. Right now, we're just investigating the accident."

She nods and looks at Joyce, but Joyce says nothing.

"Can you tell us a little about the company? Rita is the owner?"

"Yes, well, one owner. She's the founder and majority shareholder. She's the CEO and chief creative officer. There's a board of directors she has to answer to."

"But you say she's the majority shareholder? Doesn't that mean she can pretty well do whatever she wants?"

"Yes, well, she could. But she wants to keep Symbiotic happy. There's a balance there. Plus, we're looking to take the company public. Or were..."

"Who is Symbiotic?"

"They're a private equity company based in New York City. They own the other third."

"So, Rita owns two-thirds?"

"Correct."

Joyce speaks for the first time. "When did Symbiotic purchase their shares?"

Erin looks at her. "Two years ago, last Monday."

"That's very specific."

"I remember it well."

Joyce nods. "Because that's when you learned you'd move here."

Erin smiles. "Very good. The biggest shock of my life."

"You're from New York City?" Joyce asks.

"In a way. I went to NYU and stayed after college."

"You'd like to go back."

Erin reaches forward and rubs at an imaginary scuff in the wood. "Every day."

"So why move here?" Hank asks.

She sighs. "After college, I took a job with Symbiotic. They were looking to invest in more female-owned-and-operated companies." She smiles. "They thought I'd be a good fit."

"For what?" Joyce asks.

She puts a hand flat on the table and looks at it. "When they invest in a company, they like to have one of their own involved in the day-to-day."

"Like a spy?" Hank says.

Erin looks up and shakes her head quickly. "No, not at all. Rita knew full well they'd involve an employee of their own. She signed off on it."

"So, you work for them?"

"Right. I help to protect their interest in the company."

"Which is?" Joyce asks.

"Growth. They don't invest in a company without a clear plan to earn on their investment."

"How big an investment are we talking about here?" Hank asks.

"I don't know exact numbers. But at the time the company was valued at thirty million. So, a third of thirty million is ten million."

Hank lets out a low whistle, and Joyce looks around.

"How many people work here?" Joyce asks.

"In the building?"

Joyce nods.

"Three. Me, Stephanie at the front desk, and Thomas."

"You're telling me you've got a company worth thirty million dollars and only have three employees? No, excuse me, two employees and a temporary one?" Hank says.

Erin shakes her head. "No, the company has many more employees. We have a marketing team, a finance team, and others. They just don't work here. Since the pandemic, most work from home. And the company is worth far more than thirty million now."

"How much more?" Joyce asks.

"We don't know for sure. But we were set to take it public in two weeks. Projections estimated a net worth of one billion dollars."

Joyce and Hank's mouths drop open.

"A billion? With a B?" Hank asks.

Erin nods.

"So, what happens now?" Joyce asks.

"It's on hold. Without Rita, the value drops significantly. We all just hope and pray she pulls through."

The detectives nod and look at each other and then back to Erin.

"So, you've been here two years?" Joyce asks.

"Yes."

"And how do you like it?"

"Idaho?"

"Sure."

"It's okay. I miss the city, and I'm eager to go back. But I like it better than I thought I would. It's a beautiful area of the country."

"What about working here for BEAU?"

Erin looks at her, then back at her hand on the table. She clicks her nails. "It's been a growing experience."

"How so?"

"I haven't been involved with a clothing brand before."

"That's all?" Joyce asks.

Erin looks up into her eyes. "What do you mean?"

"What's your relationship been like with Rita? How do you like her?"

Erin shrugs. "She's very smart. I'm amazed by what she's accomplished."

"But?" Joyce presses.

"Let's just say I was keen for the company to go public and for Symbiotic to divest their interest in the company."

Hank looks up from his notepad. "What makes Rita so difficult?"

Erin looks at him, then at Joyce. She sighs. "Have you ever seen *The Devil Wears Prada*?"

Both shake their heads.

"Good movie, although a little too real for me now. It's about this woman who's a huge clothing designer. She's smart and successful, and everyone admires her. But she's also a tyrant. Everyone she works with hates her." Erin pauses and leans forward. "The writer of that movie knew Rita personally. She must have."

"That bad, huh?" Hank asks.

Erin shifts in her chair. "At first, it wasn't. Maybe she was on her best behavior because I was from Symbiotic, or maybe the stresses of the company got to her. But with every passing day, she got worse. She treated me and everyone else like used gum stuck to the bottom of her shoe. It got so bad about a year ago that I called Mark, my boss, and begged him to bring me back to New York. I couldn't take her anymore. I offered to do anything other than this."

"But he wouldn't let you?" Hank says.

She sighs. "No, and he was right. Rita needed me, even if she didn't think she did. I just hope they make it worth it for me."

"So...with Rita lying in a hospital bed, who runs the company?"

Erin shrugs. "Me."

Chapter 12

After leaving Erin, I stay with the detectives. They say little, preferring to listen to the rock music on the radio. That's fine with me. It gives me a chance to process what Erin had said. Was I really a tyrant? I can't hardly believe that. Something didn't seem right.

Within ten minutes, Hank pulls the vehicle into a parking space at 775 Northgate Mile. Both detectives exit the car and enter the Idaho Falls Police Department headquarters. They walk to an office that has Captain Rigby stenciled on the glass. He's on the phone, and rather than interrupt, they stand along the wall out of sight and wait. Because I have no physical limitations, I can watch them and him simultaneously.

"Yes, sir," the captain says from within the office. "As soon as I see them, sir." He hangs up and hits the intercom button on his desk phone. "Marsha, will you let Detective Powers and Gardener know I'm looking for them the second they come in?"

"They're already here."

"What?" he asks, his voice rising in pitch.

Hank and Joyce look at each other and step through the door opening.

Captain Rigby is standing behind his desk, hands on his hips. "Thank you, Marsha," he says, leaning forward and jamming the intercom button to end the call. "It's about time," he says, glaring at them. "You don't answer your phones?"

Joyce shakes her head. "I didn't see a call from you."

He looks at Hank. "What about you?"

"I was probably driving, sir."

I know this is a lie. On the drive, Joyce looked at her phone twice.

Captain Rigby crosses his arms and shakes his head, sighing. "Sit down." They take a seat opposite him. "This woman who fell yesterday. Burch. Where are we with it?"

"We're working on it," Joyce says. "We just came from her office."

"She's a bigger deal than any of us knew. I'd certainly never heard of her. The national media picked up the story. We're getting calls constantly." He was pacing behind his desk and stops. "Well? Was it an accident?"

Joyce and Hank shake their heads.

The captain's eyebrows raise. "No? Chief Henderson just called. He wants to get ahead of this. He thinks that updating the media will tamp down the excitement."

"Saying what?" Joyce asks.

"Exactly. What should he say?"

"Nothing."

The captain shakes his head. "Nope, that won't work. We've got to give them something. I guess they're camped out in front of the Burch home. One reporter tried to get into the ICU to see her this morning." Captain Rigby puts his hands on the desk and leans over it. "Someone tried to kill her?"

They nod.

I knew it!

"Who?"

Joyce upturns her hands.

"Any leads? Suspects?"

"She's the CEO of a big clothing brand," Joyce says.

The captain nods and waves a hand. "Yeah. I'd never heard of it." He motions to his computer. "I've been online this morning learning what I can about her. She's rich."

"Very. The company was valued at thirty million dollars a couple of years ago. A private equity company in New York City invested in it. They were going to take it public next week."

"So, how does that play into all this?"

"It was going to raise a billion dollars."

The captain was pacing back and forth and stops. "Billion? She's a *billionaire*?"

"She would be. Or at least pretty close once the company went public."

Captain Rigby crosses his arms and looks up at the ceiling, then turns back to them. "So, what now? Why would someone want to stop it from going public?"

Joyce puts her elbows on the armrests and steeples her fingers. "I can only think of one person. But we need to do more research."

Who? Erin? James?

Hank looks at her, furrowing his brow. "Who?"

She doesn't answer, looking at both men in turn.

"Who?" the captain says.

"Her husband. He had the most to gain."

"You think it was him?"

She nods. "I do. But maybe it wasn't his idea."

The captain frowns. "What does that mean?"

"Someone put him up to it."

Chapter 13

I watch my killer as he glances at me. My husband, James, sits in my hospital room watching the TV and occasionally glancing in my direction. Periodically, Ginger, the nurse, comes in to check something. He shouldn't be alone with me. How can this be allowed? He tried to kill me. How long will he wait to finish the job? How can the detectives leave me unguarded?

They met with their boss today and told him about James. Well...they didn't say he was a killer, exactly. They said he was the chief suspect because he had the most to gain. By killing me, he would own two-thirds of BEAU. Sure, it wasn't worth as much with me dead. But he could still sell it and get millions. But why now? Why not wait until the company went public?

Did he hate me that much? Was I that awful to live with? Was it worth possibly getting caught and seeing the value of the company drop by half just to be rid of me? If he'd stayed with me, I'd be a billionaire. Surely, I wasn't that bad to be around.

Erin hated me. That was clear from her conversation with the detectives. She described me as a villain in a movie. A year ago, she called Mark in tears, asking to be moved away from me. Why can't

I remember any of this? I don't know why, but I don't believe her story.

The door opens, and a woman pokes her head in. She looks at me, then at James. Something's familiar about her, but I can't place it. Maybe that's a good sign. Maybe my memory is coming back. James looks at her and stands, smiling.

"I wondered if you'd come," he says.

She softly closes the door and walks to him. They embrace and hold each other for several seconds. She steps back, looks up at him, then looks at me.

"I'm sorry this happened," she says.

"Me too," he says. "It still doesn't feel real. Sit down."

He motions to the seat beside him, but she ignores him, taking two steps toward me. She puts a hand on the bed's railing and looks at me. I realize why she seems familiar. She looks like me. Her hair is darker, but she has the same high cheekbones and body shape. She frowns and shakes her head, then sits in the seat beside him. "How bad is it?"

James shrugs and looks down, blowing out air. "Nothing new since yesterday. They did some tests on her before I got here, but I haven't heard the outcome."

"There are news crews out front. Is that for her?"

He nods. "They're at the house too." James looks up at her. "I didn't think you'd come, Grace."

Grace. So, that's her name.

"If she was awake, I probably wouldn't. Even though we aren't exactly close, I didn't want this to happen." She smiles for the first time.

"I'm sorry about how she treated you. I told her she was wrong, but she wouldn't hear it. I told her to apologize, but that only made her angry with me."

What is that about? What did I do to her?

Grace shrugs and sits back in her chair, then looks at him and pats his arm. "I don't know how you've done it all these years."

"What?"

She motions to my body. "Live with her."

James smiles. "It wasn't always as bad as it's been these last few years. Anyway, you lived with her almost as long."

Grace smirks. "True, you aren't the only saint."

James chuckles, and she smiles. And if I had a heart, it'd feel like someone was stabbing it with a knife.

"How are my niece and nephew? I miss seeing them. How's Paul?"

She's my sister.

Her eyes brighten. "Paul's good. He's happy teaching, and we're getting by. Rachel and Jeffery are good. They ask about you guys. They miss their cousins. Speaking of, how are the boys holding up? David's come over a few times. I don't know if you knew."

James shakes his head.

"He's not happy with his mother."

James looks at the floor. "Yeah. Yesterday was hard. None of us knows how to handle this. We're just trying to figure it out. I wasn't going to have them go to school today, but they got up on their own and wanted to go. Maybe it's good to have them doing something. Keep their minds off this."

He looks up from the floor, and their eyes lock.

"What happens?" Grace asks. "If..."

James glances at me, then back at her. "We'll sell. What else can I do? The only problem is, I don't know how. It was Rita's company, her baby. I know nothing about it. She didn't talk about it much, and I guess I didn't really ask. In a way, I resented it."

Grace pats his arm. "I don't know anything either. But Paul's smart, and we're here for you with whatever you need. I also wanted to warn you—he's going to come see you."

"Who? Paul?"

"No, *him*..."

"Oh."

"Yeah. Maybe as soon as this afternoon. I told him not to. I tried to convince him to wait, but you know how he is."

James nods, and the door opens. Dr. Mitchell stands in the doorframe. She looks different from yesterday. She's still wearing her doctor's coat, but she has heels and a skirt and wears her hair down. It's a lovely, dark color with a slight curl. She must have had a good night's sleep. She's wearing some makeup.

Grace sees her standing there and reaches for her purse. "I should go."

Dr. Mitchell holds up a hand. "No, you can stay. You're Rita's sister, right?"

Grace nods, and James reaches for her arm.

"Grace, stay, will you?"

She looks at him, then at the doctor, and sits down.

Dr. Mitchell carries over a clipboard and looks at my body, then turns back to them. "This morning, we conducted a neurological exam on Rita. Are you familiar with the Glasgow Coma Scale?"

James and Grace look at each other and shake their heads.

"The scale measures the severity of a coma. Three categories apply to the exam." She holds out three fingers and ticks them off as she speaks. "Eye response, motor response, and verbal response. Depending upon how well the patient responds to the exam, we can measure how severe the coma is. This helps us determine what care they need and also the likelihood of them waking." She pauses and looks them in the eye. "The scale ranges from three to fifteen, with three being the most severe and fifteen being the least." She stops and looks down at her clipboard. "Rita's score was a three."

James swallows, and Grace looks at him, then asks. "What does that mean?"

"It's not good. It means her eyes don't respond when tested. She obviously can't speak. And she can't move. A score of three is the lowest possible score and carries with it a high mortality rate. I'm not saying it's not possible, and I think it's too early to know for sure, but it's likely Rita will never wake up." She pauses. "I wanted to prepare you."

James swallows and nods, then looks down at the floor. Grace leans over to him and puts her arm around his back.

I have to admit, he's good. They both are. I almost believe he's sincere. Not two minutes ago, they were talking about what a witch I was.

"We'll do our best caring for her," Dr. Mitchell says. "But, at some point, you may have to decide whether you want that care to continue."

James looks up, and it's clear he understands what Dr. Mitchell is saying.

"I'm sorry," she says and leaves the room, shutting the door behind her as I realize my fate is in the hands of the person who tried to kill me.

Chapter 14

Shortly after the doctor left my bedside, James got a call. It was Joyce, the detective, and she and her partner wanted to go by the house for another look. James offered to meet them, but after he said he could remotely unlock the doors from his phone, she said there was no need. She asked if they could look around the house, and he agreed. Knowing James was expecting me to die anyway, I didn't worry about leaving him alone with my body. I concentrated my mind on Joyce and transported my consciousness to her and Hank.

They were pulling up in front of our house. Hank was behind the wheel, and Joyce was surveying the neighborhood. Hank put the car in park, pushed the ignition button, and both detectives exited.

It's a beautiful late spring day in Southern Idaho. The mountains are still capped with snow, but blossoms are in the trees, and birds are singing.

Joyce walks to the head of the driveway and stops looking at the house. Hank joins her.

"When we talked to James, he said that Rita rang the doorbell that morning."

Hank looks down at his notepad, then back up at the house. "Right."

"Why? He said she didn't normally do that. Why didn't she pull into the garage?"

"I don't know."

"Will you go into the house and open the garage?"

"Sure."

Hank walks up the steps leading to the house, opens the door, and disappears. After a few seconds, the garage door opens, and he comes out. Joyce walks down the driveway past him and opens the driver's door to the Mercedes. She looks up and pushes the button of the auxiliary garage door opener attached to the visor. The overhead opener engages and shuts. She waits until it closes completely, then reaches over to the middle of the ceiling where the car's built-in garage door opener is. Three buttons protrude from the area, and she pushes each. A different garage door opens with each button.

"Hmm," Joyce says. She exits the car and moves over to the only other vehicle in the garage. She opens the door and struggles to get into the driver's seat because of her height.

"Need a boost?" Hank says, smiling.

She gives him a look, then checks the ceiling of the truck cab and pushes the buttons on the built-in garage door openers. Just like the Mercedes, they each open a different garage door. Joyce climbs down from the truck and closes the door. She goes back to the Mercedes and tries the external garage door remote. Again, it opens the garage door directly behind the vehicle.

"Why didn't it work yesterday?" Hank asks.

Joyce looks at him. "Exactly. Let's go look around the house."

For the next twenty minutes, they wander the house, looking in each bedroom, opening drawers, and reading the mail. Eventually, they go outside to the backyard and walk around the patio, occasionally stopping but not saying much to each other. Finally, they reenter the house and stand in the kitchen.

"Did you make a note of Rita's number?"

Hank nods and flips through the notepad. He reads it aloud to Joyce while she dials. Joyce walks upstairs while Hank stays on the main level. She dials the number repeatedly but doesn't hear a sound. After a few minutes, Joyce comes back downstairs.

"It must be on silent. The cellphone towers put the phone here."

Joyce walks down the hall and reenters the garage with Hank on her tail. She dials the number again and opens the door to the Mercedes. They hear a buzzing. Hank opens the passenger door, and they search the car. Finally, Hank opens the back door and tells Joyce to move the driver's side seat forward. He reaches under the seat and pulls out a pink phone with a large *B* on the back and home screen. He holds it up to show Joyce.

"Let's go get that over to the lab," Joyce says.

They exit the garage. Hank closes the overhead door by touching the ENTER button on the keypad, and they walk to their car. Before opening the door, Joyce stops and looks around.

"Where does Kim live?" Joyce asks.

Hank looks down and reviews his notepad. He looks up and points to a house three down from ours on the same side of the street. "There."

Rather than get in the car, Joyce walks along the sidewalk and stops in front of Kim's house. She stares at it.

"What are you looking at?" Hank asks.

Joyce bites the inside of her cheek. She pulls out her phone and takes a picture of the home, then turns back to Hank. She shakes her head and starts walking back to our house, and Hank walks with her. "Are you going to tell me what that was about?"

She looks up at him, then stops. "How much does a house in this neighborhood run?"

He looks around at the finely landscaped homes. No house is less than five thousand square feet. "At least a million. Some, probably double that."

"Fair to say it's an exclusive neighborhood?"

"Absolutely."

Joyce nods. "What about your neighborhood? Would you say it's exclusive?"

Hank chuckles. "Surely, you jest."

"When was your house built?"

Hank shrugs. "Maybe five years ago."

"So pretty new."

"Yeah."

"Aside from the size of the houses and the fine landscaping, what else is different from your neighborhood?"

Hank looks around, examining the houses again. Finally, he shakes his head.

"Tonight, when you go home, look closely at the houses. I bet you'll find that one in every four or five looks the same. Same floor plan, same layout. If you were to go into the houses, you'd have a hard time telling them apart." She pauses and points across the street. "This neighborhood is different. Rich people don't want their houses to resemble their neighbors'. They want a custom design. All the houses look different. Except two." She points at our house and then at Kim's.

Hank's mouth drops open. "So, what does it—"

"Are you the detectives investigating the murder of Rita Burch?'

Hank and Joyce turn to see an elderly couple in tracksuits walking toward them, both wearing tennis shoes with large soles. The man wears a red-white-and-blue sweatband. The woman is in the brightest neon yellow imaginable.

"I'm sorry?" Joyce says as they approach.

"Rita Burch," the woman demands. She's a willow of a woman. Tall and narrow. Her unnaturally brown hair is wispy. "Are you investigating who tried to kill her? On the news this morning, they said it wasn't an accident. Someone pushed her off the balcony."

Joyce eyes her. "We're investigating what happened to her. Yes."

"Oh, don't tell me it was an accident," the woman says. "I'm no fool."

"Do you have something you'd like to tell us, ma'am?" Hank says.

The woman cranes her neck to look up at him. Her husband does the same.

"Her husband killed her."

"You know that?"

She waves a hand. "It's him. Nobody that nice could be with someone that awful. At some point, they have to snap. Nasty woman. As far as I'm concerned, she got what was coming to her."

Another one?

"You don't like Rita?"

She shakes her head and points to her husband. "You know she called the police on Larry for mowing the lawn? Can you imagine such a thing? It was right after they moved in. Just days before, we'd taken them cookies. She never thanked us or even waved. And then, she had the gall to call the police on us. If you ask me, which you haven't, she had it coming. I don't know how her husband lived with her. And those poor kids..." She shakes her head. "Come on, Larry." She grabs her husband's arm and pulls him along.

Hank and Joyce watch as they walk inside the house next to ours. When the door shuts, Joyce removes her cell phone from the holster on her belt and dials a number.

"Sarah?" she says into the phone after a pause. "Can you come out to the Burch home? We found her cell phone and want to get it analyzed. We'd bring it by the station, but something's come up. We need to stay around here a little longer."

Chapter 15

The detectives sit in their car waiting for Sarah, and my curiosity focuses back on James. He sits alone on the bleachers at Mountain Ridge Junior High. The gymnasium is full of athletes, cheerleaders, students, and parents. After sitting down, several parents make their way over to him and offer condolences. Others steal glances in his direction, whispering and wondering if he tried to kill me.

Our youngest son, Reed, stands on the court, hand over his chest, as the national anthem is sung. He's easy to identify because of his long, curly, blond hair. His older brother also stands on the court. He's singing the anthem along with three other boys from the school's choir.

When they finish, the crowd cheers and the boys head over to the bench for last-minute instructions. Gilbert separates from the other singers and walks up the bleachers to his dad.

"Dad, do you mind if I sit with my friends for a few minutes?"

James shakes his head. "That's fine, buddy."

Gilbert turns away, then stops and looks back at James. Making up his mind, he sits down beside him.

James looks at him. "You can go. I'll be okay."

"No, I want to stay with you."

James smiles and looks over at Reed. He's sitting on the bench, not starting this game. James watches him, and Reed puts his hands up in a shrug. It's obvious he's not happy about sitting out to start the game.

The game begins, and Mountain Ridge falls behind by ten points. Midway through the first quarter, a man in his sixties enters the gymnasium and surveys the crowd. His eyes stop on James, and he walks in his direction. He climbs the stairs when James notices him. The man stops in front of him.

"Hi, James."

James watches him. "Hi, Steve."

Who is this guy? Again, something about him is familiar.

"Mind if I sit down?"

James shakes his head, and Steve sits beside him. He looks at Gilbert. "Hey there, Donovan. Look at how you've grown."

Gilbert looks at his dad, then at Steve. "I'm Gilbert."

"Oh, that's right," he says. He reaches over and pats his arm. "It's been too long since I've seen my grandsons."

He's my father. Grace warned James he'd come. But why did she warn him?

Gilbert nods, and they all turn to watch the game. Reed kneels at the scorer's table, waiting to check-in.

"Which one is Reed?" the man asks James.

James points him out.

"Oh, that's right. I still wonder where he got that blond hair. Makes you wonder, huh?" He chuckles, but James only glares at him. "Nobody on our side of the family has blonde hair."

James keeps his eyes on the game.

The whistle blows, and the referee motions to Reed. He comes into the game and makes an impact, getting a steal and finding another player for a layup on a great assist.

"How are you doing?" Steve asks.

"Hanging in there," James says, keeping his eyes on the game.

"I went by the hospital and then the house. One of the older boys told me you were here. I saw Rita, and she didn't look good. What do the doctors say?"

There's a timeout in the game, and James turns to him. "What do you mean?"

"It looks to me like the machines are keeping her alive."

James leans over to Gilbert. "Hey, buddy, can you give me and your grandpa a few minutes? Maybe you could go sit with your friends."

Gilbert looks at his dad, then his grandpa, and nods. He gets up and joins a group of boys at the other end of the bleachers. James turns back, sighing. "What do you want me to say?"

"I'm just saying, it looks like you're just delaying the inevitable. Maybe you should think about shutting off the machines. I know it's hard. She's my daughter. But she's suffering."

James turns back to the game.

"Don't you think it would be better for the boys?"

James shakes his head. "You don't even know them."

"Only because Rita wouldn't let me."

"And why was that?"

Steve looks at him in surprise. They fall silent, watching the activity on the court. Reed makes a three-pointer and both men cheer. The buzzer sounds, and the teams huddle for halftime.

"Look, I know I wasn't the best father for my girls. You're ten times the father I ever was. But the boys need to move on, and so do you. Seeing her rot away in a hospital bed is prolonging the closure you need." He puts a hand on James's shoulder. "Just think about it."

James doesn't respond, and they watch the rest of the game. When it finishes, they wait for Reed to congratulate the other team, then go meet him on the court. James hugs him, and Steve goes for a high five. "Great game out there, champ. You must have gotten your three-point shooting from your grandpa and mom. We were both pretty impressive athletes in our day."

Wow, he actually said something nice about me. It doesn't mean much, considering he wants the machines turned off and for me to die.

Reed smiles, and they all walk out of the gym together. As they get close to James's Tahoe, my father speaks to Reed and Gilbert. "Boys, can you give me a second with your dad?"

The boys nod and go climb in the car. When the doors shut, Steve says to James, "I hate to ask. I know you're going through a lot right now. But I need some help."

James looks at him and sighs. "How much?"

"Could you do a thousand?"

"A thousand?"

"I know. It's more than I've ever asked. But at least you don't have to hide it from Rita now."

So, that's it. James has been giving him money behind my back.

James looks him in the eye and shakes his head. Finally, he shrugs. "It'll be in your account tomorrow."

My father wraps his arms around him. "Thank you, James. I love you."

James pulls away and pats him on the shoulder, then gets into the Tahoe.

Chapter 16

Curious about the detectives, I focus my mind back on them and find them standing in front of a custom front door while the doorbell flashes lights in a circular motion. After a few seconds, a voice emanates from the speaker.

"Yes, can I help you?"

"Hi, my name is Hank Gardener, and this is Joyce Powers. We're detectives with the Idaho Falls Police Department." Hank shows his badge to the camera. "Are you Kim Long?"

"Yes."

"Mrs. Long, can we speak with you?"

"I'm at the grocery store. I'll be home in five minutes."

"That's fine. We'll wait."

Hank steps back from the house and walks to the bottom of the cement stairs. He looks up at the roof while Joyce watches him. After several seconds, he bites his cheek and climbs the steps to stand beside Joyce.

"Do you know what Jensen said when he learned I was your partner?"

"What?"

"That I didn't look enough like Dr. Watson."

Joyce rolls her eyes. "I guess that's better than being called Miss Marple."

Hank smiles. "Nah, you never wear a dress and hat."

A white Jeep Wagoneer pulls into the driveway, and the overhead garage door opens. Hank and Joyce walk down the steps leading to the front door and meet Kim as she climbs out of the vehicle in the garage. Aside from the Wagoneer, the garage is virtually empty, other than a bicycle and a stack of identical shipping boxes.

Hank steps to her, extending his hand. "Detective Hank Gardener," he says, then motions to Joyce. "And this is my partner, Detective Joyce Powers."

Kim shakes their hands, then slips past them to the back of the SUV and opens it. "Sorry, I need to get these groceries inside. I've got ice cream."

Hank steps closer. "Let me help you with those."

She thanks him, and he takes four bags to a hand and carries a gallon of milk between his fingers in the right. Kim picks up the other gallon.

"Are you sure you don't want me to take some of those?" Kim asks.

"No, I've got them. You just lead me where you want me to go."

Kim smiles and steps in front of him, and Hank follows. Joyce lingers, looking inside the car and examining the garage, going so far as to open one of the boxes. Kim shows Hank to the kitchen, and he places the bags and milk on the large island countertop.

"Have a seat over there," she says, pointing to the family room off the kitchen. "I'll just get these put away and be right with you."

"Sounds good," Hank says and turns to see Joyce hasn't joined them yet. He moves over and sits on the couch. After a minute, Joyce enters and sits beside him. Eventually, Kim returns and takes a seat opposite them in an oversized lounge chair better suited to Hank than her.

"So," she says, crossing her legs and sitting back. She's wearing black leggings, tennis shoes, and a tight tank top that reveals a generous amount of cleavage. I don't think she wears a top that doesn't highlight her financial investment. "Is this about Rita? I saw both of you in the hospital the other day."

Hank nods while Joyce says nothing, letting him guide the conversation. "We understand you know the family well."

Kim smiles. "Probably the best of anyone around here. Rita and I are friends. Probably her only friend. We work out together, and Reed plays on the basketball team with my son, Spencer."

"How long have you known her?"

"Maybe six months. She started coming to the same gym after they moved in. We quickly figured out we were neighbors."

Hank tries to be subtle, but I watch his eyes dart to her left hand. She's not wearing a ring. Kim sees it and holds her left hand out toward him. "No ring. I'm divorced."

"I'm sorry."

"Don't be. I'm not. It's the best thing that could have happened to me. My ex-husband was a real piece of work. Now if he'd only agree to the alimony."

"Bitter divorce, huh?"

She guffaws. "You could say that."

"Do you work outside the home?"

"Part-time at a dental office. It's hard with the kids."

Hank motions to the pictures on the wall. "How old are they?"

She turns to check the pictures, then back to him. "Spencer's thirteen and Emily's nine."

"Cute kids," Hank says.

"Thank you. Do you have any?"

"Not yet. Maybe someday."

She looks at Joyce.

"I do but grown," Joyce says.

"How long have you been divorced?" Hank asks.

"He left five months ago. As far as the state of Idaho goes, we're still married. But it's just a matter of time."

"I see," Hank says.

"Can you tell us about the Burches?" Joyce says.

"What do you want to know?"

"Anything that comes to mind. How do you know them and any impressions you have?"

"Can I ask a question first?"

"Sure," Joyce says.

"Was Rita's fall an accident?"

Joyce looks at Hank, then back to Kim.

"I only ask, because the TV is saying it wasn't. I had a reporter stop me outside my house this morning."

Joyce looks at her closely. "We haven't ruled out any possibilities, but whoever reported that didn't talk to us."

Kim nods. "So, is that a yes or a no?"

"What do you think?" Joyce says.

Kim shrugs.

"Let's just say we're investigating all possibilities."

"Fair enough," Kim says.

"You said you were Rita's friend. Maybe her only friend. Why do you say that?"

Kim smiles. "If you knew Rita, you'd know why."

"Explain it to us," Joyce says.

"She could be difficult. I loved her, but she wasn't exactly patient."

"Do you know if someone wanted to hurt her?"

Kim chuckles and raises a hand. "Everyone who met her. Look, I loved Rita. But...I can't say others felt the same." Kim bobs her head. "The thing is, Rita was really smart. I mean, *really* smart. And someone like that, sometimes, doesn't have the most patience with others. They think everyone should have a brain like theirs. Rita could figure things out so fast. Her brain was like a computer. One time, at the gym, the trainer got pretty frustrated with her."

"Oh?"

"Yeah. This girl kept asking questions and Rita lost it. She walked over, took the remote from the instructor, told the girl to go to the global gym, and started the clock. It got heated between the girl and Rita. The trainer had to separate them."

"What was the girl's name?"

"I don't know. I never saw her again."

Nobody speaks, and Kim fills the silence. "You know her company was about to go public, right?"

"Yes," Joyce says.

"She was going to be the richest person anyone around here could imagine." Kim sits forward in her chair, dropping her voice to a whisper. "Do you think it's related?"

"What?" Hank asks.

"Her fall."

Hank says, "Do you?"

Kim looks up at the ceiling. "I don't know. I mean...something keeps running around my head since I heard the news."

"What's that?"

Kim leans forward. "Rita didn't want to take the company public?"

Hank and Joyce look at each other, and then Hank speaks. "No?"

Kim leans back and shakes her head.

"She told you that?"

Kim nods. "She said the company wasn't ready yet. She said the girl in her office was pressuring her, and that was coming from New York."

"Did Rita ever say if she feared anyone? If she was ever worried about her safety?"

"No, never."

"Who else did Rita not get along with?" Joyce asks.

"I'm not exaggerating when I say it seemed like everyone. None of the neighbors liked her. She wasn't friendly. Several claimed she called the police on them for stupid things." She snaps her fingers. "Have you checked into the equity guy?"

"What equity guy?" Joyce asks.

"The one from New York. The one who bought part of the company."

"Should we?" Hank asks.

She scoffs. "I think so."

"Why?" Joyce says.

"Rita was always saying he wanted her to do things differently in her company. They would fight a lot about it. Rita wanted him out. He's the one who was pushing to take it public."

"Hmm," Joyce says. "Did she say anything else about him?"

Kim looks up at the ceiling. "I think his name was Mark. He seemed to only care about money."

"Thanks for the tip. What about James?" Joyce says.

"What about him?"

"Were there problems in their marriage?"

Kim frowns and shakes her head. "No, not that she ever said to me. She'd get frustrated with him sometimes. You know what I was saying about patience. But I think she loved him."

"What about him? Do you think he could have hurt her?" Hank asks.

"What do you mean?"

"Been physical with her."

She laughs. "Are you kidding? Do you know James? You've met him, right? He's seriously the nicest guy. All the neighbors, kids, everyone loves him. No way he'd ever hurt her. You're wasting your time looking into him."

Hmm.

Hank leans back in his chair. "If someone caused her accident, who would it be?"

Kim shakes her head. "I've been thinking about that. Lots of people hated her, but I don't think anyone would hurt her. Unless maybe that Mark guy. You know, the more I think about it, the more I think Rita did it to herself."

What?

Joyce sits forward. "Why do you say that? Did she try to hurt herself before?"

Kim shrugs. "No, not that I know of. But I don't know... Just a feeling, really. Rita was always working, and she put so much pressure on herself. She could never relax. I think it finally got to her. With the company being pushed public and the pressure she was getting from Mark. She felt like the only thing she could control was slipping away from her. I think she finally snapped."

Joyce looks at Hank, and he nods, standing. "Thank you, Mrs. Long. We appreciate your help today."

Kim stands with them. "You can call me Kim. Let me walk you out."

Kim goes in front, and they walk behind her. When they reach the front door, Kim opens it, and they step outside and turn back to her, extending their hands. They all shake, and the two detectives turn away, and then Joyce stops.

"Kim, sorry, one more question. Where were you at the time of the accident?"

Kim frowns. "Why?"

Joyce waves a hand. "Oh, no reason. We're asking everyone."

Kim looks at her, then at Hank. "I was getting my kids off to school."

"Driving them?"

She puts a finger to her lips. "No, I think James took them that day. Actually, he took the oldest, Spencer. My daughter went a few minutes later. She's still in elementary. I drove her, then rushed back. I had to be to work at nine. I remember hearing the sirens."

"So, you were here at home?"

She nods. "Yeah, when the ambulance came, I was just getting in the shower. I didn't hear them long and didn't check."

"So, you didn't know they stopped at the Burch home?"

"No."

Chapter 17

After leaving Kim's house, I decide to stay with the detectives. Learning that I didn't want to take the company public left me wondering where they might go next. The location was a surprise. Hank and Joyce enter Skyline High School and head to the main office, which is empty, save for a girl sitting behind a desk. She looks young enough to be a student.

"Hi, can I help you?" she says. She has light-auburn hair and a sprinkling of freckles along the bridge of her nose.

"Hello," Hank says. "Is the principal in?"

"Let me check."

She picks up a phone on the desk and dials a number. "Mr. Skinner? Two people are here to see you." She pauses as she listens. "He wants to know what this is regarding."

"Tell him we're detectives from the Idaho Falls Police Department."

The girl's eyes widen, and she repeats the message. She listens, occasionally nodding, then puts down the receiver. "He'll be right with you."

A door opens from down the hall, and a tall man, at least six-two, exits the office and approaches. "Detectives," he says.

"Principal Skinner, I'm Detective Hank Gardener, and this is Detective Joyce Powers."

Skinner smiles and shakes their hands. "Thank you for coming so quickly. It's just right out here." Skinner walks out of the office, holding the door open. Hank gives Joyce a look and she shrugs. They follow him out. "We've seen vandalism before, but this is getting to be too much, too often. This is the fourth time this week."

The principal motions ahead, and they walk down the wide hallway. When they reach two-thirds of the way down, he stops and points. One locker is caved in. Joyce and Hank step closer, surveying the damage.

"When did you notice this?" Joyce asks.

"This afternoon."

"About what time?"

"I don't know. Maybe about three."

"Does the locker still open?"

The principal nods and pulls on the handle. The locker swings open, but it's empty.

"Most of the lockers are empty. Kids don't really use lockers anymore. They carry everything in their backpacks."

Joyce nods and walks across the hall to a classroom. She looks inside. Maps cover the walls. She looks at the whiteboard in the front, then returns to the principal, pointing. "Was that the second locker vandalized?"

Skinner nods. "How'd you know that?"

"Can you show us where the first was?"

"The first and third are in the same location, just like these."

He walks them to the other side of the school. The lockers look just like the first two. Joyce motions to the first locker.

What is this? Why are they wasting their time on this? Someone tried to kill me, and they're investigating high school lockers?

"Mr. Skinner, will you make a fist for me?" Skinner balls up his right hand, and Joyce asks him to put it in the dent in the locker. "When did you say you first noticed this dent?"

"Around three last Friday."

Joyce looks at the other locker, then walks across the hall and looks inside the room. A teacher sits behind the desk. Joyce approaches, keeping her voice low.

"Is David Burch in any of your classes?"

Ah ha...

The woman looks up, pushing her glasses up her nose.

"What?"

"David Burch, is he a student of yours?"

"Yes, he's in my second period."

"When does the second period end?"

"About ten thirty."

"Has David been coming in early or staying late? Maybe last week?"

"Yes. How did you know that?"

"Maybe Friday?"

"Yes, he's been late too many times and has an unsatisfactory on his citizenship. He's been doing chores around the classroom to make it up. He's not happy about it."

Joyce smiles, thanks her, and walks out, meeting Skinner and Hank at the vandalized lockers.

"Well, we'll need to file a police report on this. If you find out who's been doing it, let us know. We'll open an investigation."

Both men look at her, and Joyce stares at Hank.

"Anyway," Hank says to Skinner, "you might want to offer some kind of reward to the other students. Maybe someone saw something."

Skinner nods. "That's a good idea."

"While we're here," Joyce says, "I'm sure you've heard about the accident of Rita Burch, the mother of two students?"

Skinner nods.

"We're working on something for the family and need to check their attendance records. Who should we talk to?"

"Jim Roberts is our school guidance counselor. He can help you."

Skinner walks them back to the front of the building and shows them to Dr. Roberts's office. Dr. Roberts, a severely overweight man with large glasses and thinning hair, greets them. His office is full of binders, and stacks of paper cover his desk. After they introduce themselves, they sit down opposite the desk from him.

"Mr. Skinner said you could help us check attendance records for two students here."

Roberts nods.

"Can you print the attendance records for David and Donovan Burch for the last couple of weeks?"

"Sure," Roberts says. He moves his mouse and types on the keyboard. Seconds later, the printer starts up. He follows the same steps, and when the printing stops, he swivels around in his chair, grabs the papers, and hands them to Joyce. "Is there something I can answer for you? Is this related to their mother?"

Joyce nods and looks down at the papers in her hands. David's transcript is on top, and she sees multiple tardies, but otherwise, his attendance has been stellar. She flips to the next page, and Donovan's transcript is much different. She looks up at Dr. Roberts.

"The kid hasn't been to school in three weeks."

"He hasn't?"

Joyce frowns. "Has anyone called the home? Do the parents know?"

Roberts looks at his monitor and strikes a few keys. "His father has been excusing the absences. The kid's been sick."

Joyce looks at Hank and stands. "Thank you, Dr. Roberts."

Chapter 18

The detectives make a phone call when they get back to their car, updating the captain on their progress. I take the opportunity to check on my family. The boys are at home, and James is still at the hospital. I decide to get back to the detectives and join them as Hank pulls the Dodge Charger into the parking lot of Teton Toyota and parks in one of the customer parking spaces.

"Do you think he's here?" Hank asks Joyce.

Joyce shrugs. "Let's go look around the lot. It won't be long until a sales associate finds us."

They exit the car, and Hank follows Joyce over to the line of Tacomas on the north side of the building. She stops in front of an aqua-blue one.

"Do you like trucks?" she asks Hank.

He stands beside her, admiring the vehicle. "I do. I like the headroom."

She looks up at him and smiles.

"I'd prefer one of those, though." He points to the row of Tundras, Toyota's full-size trucks. "Even more room."

Joyce shakes her head. "Men and trucks...," she says and walks around to the driver's door. On the window is a fact sheet, including the MSRP price. She whistles. "Forty-five thousand dollars?" She looks at him and he nods.

"I bet the Tundras are more."

"How much more?"

He shrugs. "Probably another five to ten grand."

Joyce shakes her head and tries the door. It's locked.

"Welcome to Teton Toyota," a voice says from behind them.

They turn to see a man with a goatee standing a few feet away. He's wearing a cowboy hat and a golf shirt with the company logo on the left breast.

"My name's John Wayne, but you can just call me John. Are you in the market for a new Tacoma? Sounds like you might want to upgrade to the Tundra?"

Joyce steps away from the Tacoma and looks down the line of trucks.

"My husband wants a truck. I'm not sure what kind."

John looks at her and then at Hank, trying to establish the relationship.

"We work together," Hank says, winking.

John laughs. "You never know."

Joyce is still looking at the trucks. "We came by before. A guy by the name of Steve helped us out. He asked for us to request him if we came again."

Joyce isn't watching as John's face falls.

"He's here today. I'll send him over."

John strides away, and Joyce walks to the Tundras. Hank follows. She stops in front of the dark green model and looks up at Hank. "What do you think of that one?"

Hank nods. "I like it. I like the crew cab better. But I like it." He points to the truck beside the one she's referring to.

"The black one?"

"Eh, I like the dark green better. But I like the size of the cab."

She walks to the side of it, frowning. "But the bed is shorter."

"So?"

"So, what if the dead bodies are as tall as you?"

He laughs as my father walks up to them.

"I'm Steve," he says, looking at them. He's attempting to place them but trying to hide it.

"Hi, Steve. I'm Joyce. Do you remember me?"

Steve nods. "I think so..."

"I was here with my husband, Sam, a few weeks back. I'm looking to buy him a truck as a birthday present and wondered if I could take this one for a test drive?"

My father looks at her, then at Hank. "Sure. I'll just need a copy of your license. I need to get the keys."

Joyce has her license ready and hands it to him. He looks at it. "Great. I'll be right back."

He walks away, and Joyce returns to the green truck.

"Is Sam serious about getting a truck?" Hank asks.

"Unfortunately," Joyce says, getting on tiptoes and cupping her hands to shade the glass. "I'm not going to tell him about this. He'd be more excited than our wedding night." Hank laughs. She looks at him. "Does that say more about him? Or me?"

My father returns with the keys to the black truck and opens it up. He puts a license in the window and holds the door open.

Joyce turns to Hank. "Wanna drive?"

"Sure," Hank says and walks around to the driver's side.

Steve sputters like a teakettle.

"I promise, he's qualified," she says, showing him her badge.

"Oh," he says, his eyes going wide. "Do you want to take it alone?"

"Nah," Joyce says. "Come along. You can ride in the bed."

He shakes his head, then stops and smiles when she does. She climbs in the passenger's side, and he gets in the row behind her. Hank has his seat adjusted and after a few seconds pulls out of the parking space and exits the parking lot.

"Steve, how's your daughter?" Joyce asks.

She's turned in her seat so she can look at him.

"Grace?"

Joyce frowns. "No, Rita."

"Oh." He sees Hank looking at him in the rearview mirror and looks back at Joyce. "Is that why you're here?" Joyce says nothing, only watches him. My father hesitates. "I went and saw her yesterday."

"Good. And?"

"She's not in good shape."

Joyce's look goes hard. "Did you have anything to do with her accident?"

My father's face goes white. "No," he stammers.

Joyce doesn't respond. She continues to stare at him.

"What? I didn't."

"She blames you for what happened to her mother."

He looks down.

"We know you've asked her for money several times. She hasn't responded. That had to make you mad."

Do they know James has been giving him money?

"Not mad. Disappointed..."

"Has James been helping you out? Giving you money? That's a lot of debt."

His eyes dart between her and Hank. Finally, he looks down. "Yes."

"How often?"

"Maybe once a month. I try not to ask but..."

"How much does he give you?"

"Only a few hundred, mostly. Just enough to help with my rent if I don't sell enough here."

"Where were you Tuesday morning between seven-thirty and nine?"

"Home."

"Alone?"

"Yes."

Joyce clicks her tongue. "You aren't helping your case, Steve. Your son-in-law has been giving you money because your daughter won't. You've got a mountain of debt. It seems like life would be better for you without Rita. It's not helping that you have no alibi for the time of the accident."

My father extends a palm. "Listen, I didn't hurt my daughter. Yes, I asked her for money, and she hasn't given me any. James has helped because he's a good kid. I know she hates me for what I did. I hate myself. I wish things were different. But I'd never hurt her, not physically."

Joyce continues staring at him, then looks at Hank. "This really is a nice truck, isn't it?"

Hank nods, pulling back into the dealership parking lot.

"Do you want it back in the same spot?" Hank asks.

"Uh... You can just park in one of the customer spots. I'll have one of the lot techs put it back."

Hank does as he asks. When he shuts off the car, they all climb out.

Joyce looks at my father and expels a large breath. "I'll get back to you on the truck. That's a lot of money."

Steve nods, and Hank hands him the keys. He stands still, looking at them, then turns away when Joyce calls him back.

"Steve, do you like to iron?"

"Iron?"

"Yeah, iron clothes." Joyce mimes the motion.

He looks at Hank for an explanation. Hank doesn't give him one.

"Uh...no."

"You never iron?"

"I have an iron, but I don't use it much."

"Do you ever wear dress shirts? Something a little fancier than the logo golf shirts?"

He shrugs. "Sometimes."

"Don't you iron them?"

He shakes his head. "I get the wrinkle-free kind."

Joyce eyes him, and his cheek twitches. "Thank you, Steve. I hope you sell a car today."

Chapter 19

After leaving the dealership, I stay with Hank and Joyce as they drive through the middle of town and pass the falls on their way to a neighborhood of modest homes. Joyce points to a small split-entry home. Something feels familiar about the house, but I can't place it. Hank pulls the car to the curb in front of the house and shuts off the engine. The home has brown brick with yellow siding. The brick is only on the front. The lawn has been maintained, and there's a small flowerbed under the front window. Four cement steps lead to the white front door. Brass numbers, 2677, hang from the brick beside the entrance. The doorbell's old school, a simple button in a brass fixture. Hank presses the button, and both detectives stand on the porch looking at the cul-de-sac across the street.

"A little different from her sister's neighborhood, huh?" Joyce says.

Hank nods.

"Look down there. Second house on the right."

Hank surveys the home.

"Same floor plan as this one."

Hank nods, and they turn back to the door as it opens. A small woman in her late thirties holds the door open, looking at them. A small dog yaps behind her.

"Yes, can I help you?"

"Grace?" Hank asks.

"Yes."

Both detectives reach inside their pockets and pull out their badges.

"My name is Detective Gardener. This is Detective Powers. We're from Idaho Falls PD. Do you have a few minutes to talk with us?"

She looks up at Hank, then down at Joyce. They smile and she shrugs. "You can come in, I guess." She pulls the door open wide, and both detectives step inside. The landing is small, and there's barely room for Grace to shut the door. Hank has to press himself into the wall. "Sorry," she says, squeezing past him. She walks up the seven steps to the main level of the house and waves for them to follow.

The hallway and living room have no wall separating them. There's a couch and a loveseat under the window. The fabric is frayed on the couch, and there's a large red stain on the carpet in the middle of the room. Grace waves to the couch.

"Have a seat. I'm just helping my daughter get changed. I'll be right back."

They nod, and she walks up the four stairs to the top part of the house. She disappears down the hall, and they look around. The home is modest, probably less than sixteen hundred square feet. There's an archway that connects the kitchen to the front room.

A sliding glass door opens from the kitchen to a small red deck. A swing set is visible in the backyard.

Voices at the stairs bring back their attention. Grace holds a small child, no older than five, in her arms. The girl has no hair. A tube runs from her nostrils down into an oxygen tank. Mother and child struggle down the stairs. When they reach the level of the detectives, Grace puts down the oxygen tank and drags it while holding the child against her hip.

She enters the room, and the little girl looks at the detectives. Hank swallows, and Joyce smiles at her. Her enormous eyes examine them with curiosity.

"Sorry," Grace says, a little out of breath. She places the girl on the loveseat, arranges the oxygen tank, and sits down beside her. Hank and Joyce look at each other, then back at mother and daughter.

"What's your name?" Joyce asks the little girl.

"Rachel," the girl says.

"That's a pretty name. How old are you, Rachel?"

She smiles. "Five." She holds up a hand with all her fingers extended.

Joyce shakes her head. "What a wonderful age. I'm five too. Except, there's another five in my age. There are two fives. So, we're pretty much the same."

Rachel looks at her mom and giggles. Grace smiles and nods at her daughter. She pulls a tablet with a pink case from beside the couch and hands it to Rachel. Rachel adjusts it in her small hands.

"Honey, these people are detectives. They want to talk to me for a few minutes." She hands Rachel a set of headphones. "Can you watch one of your shows while we talk?"

Rachel nods and puts on the headphones, careful not to disturb the oxygen tube with the cord.

Grace turns back to the detectives.

"How long ago was she diagnosed?" Joyce asks.

Grace sighs. "Eight months ago. Leukemia."

Hank swallows and says nothing, leaving the conversation to Joyce.

"How did you know?" Joyce asks.

"We noticed her balance was off. She was getting tired too fast and too often. She's always been so active, and she became lethargic. She just wanted to sit around all the time. So, we took her in. They diagnosed it pretty quickly. She just finished a round of chemo. So far, so good." Grace forces a smile. There's a moment of silence as the women look at each other. Finally, Grace asks, "So, what can I help you with?"

Joyce looks at Hank, and he clears his throat. When he speaks, his voice is soft. "We wanted to talk to you about Rita."

"I figured. What about her?"

"You know about her accident?"

She nods. "James called me yesterday. I went to the hospital to see her."

Hank looks at Joyce, then back to Grace. He hesitates. "We understand you two aren't close."

Grace shrugs. "That depends on the time frame. Growing up, we were very close. She's only a few years older. We did everything together. In the last three years...we haven't spoken."

"What happened?"

"Four years ago, our father cheated on our mother. Not long after, our mother died quite literally of a broken heart. Her heart stopped beating. Rita and I didn't see things the same way."

"How so?" Hank asks.

"I don't know if it's because of my name or religious beliefs, but I found it easier to forgive our father. My forgiveness incensed Rita. She claimed forgiving him meant I was turning my back on our mother." Grace stops and looks out the window. "Our mother's funeral was the last time I saw Rita until yesterday in the hospital." After a pause, she looks at the detectives. "Was my sister's fall an accident?"

Hank hesitates.

"No," Joyce says.

The two women stare at each other for a beat.

"Someone tried to kill her?"

"We believe so."

Grace raises a finger and rubs at her cheek. A line creases her forehead.

"We're talking to anyone close to her. Anyone who might help with our investigation."

"As I told you, we haven't talked in three years. I doubt I can tell you much."

"Your sister was a wealthy woman," Joyce says and looks at Rachel. "Did she help?"

Grace lets out her breath in a cough. "She didn't even know. Our father tried to tell her, but she wouldn't talk to him."

"Did that make you angry?" Joyce asks.

"What? Mad enough to kill her?" Grace shakes her head. "No."

Joyce looks around. "I'm not wanting to offend, but I have to say, if my sister was a multimillionaire and my child had cancer, I'd be furious if she wouldn't help."

Grace nods. "I'd be lying if I said I wasn't hurt. At times, I was beyond angry. I couldn't believe the person she became. It was as if I didn't know her anymore. Her oldest, David, has visited from time to time. He's told me about her. He won't even call her mom. It changed my perspective. I went from hating her to pitying her. You know, the thing they say about grudges is true. It becomes a poison inside you. I saw what it did to Rita. Her hatred toward our father poisoned her. She changed from the person she was."

"Did James know?"

"About Rachel?"

"Yes."

Grace nods. "He never talked to me about it, but he must have known. In fact," she looks back out the window, "we had a couple of large donations come through our church. I've wondered if they came from him. He's never said, and I've never asked. He's a good man."

"Again, I hope you don't think me indelicate, but I have to ask. How are your finances?"

Grace shrugs. "Well, I don't have a house like my sister, if that's what you mean. But because of the generosity of others, we've gotten by. We're doing okay. We'll get through this."

"Two more questions, then we'll go."

Grace nods.

"Where were you Tuesday morning between seven forty-five and eight thirty?"

"At a doctor's appointment for Rachel."

"Doctor's name?"

"Dr. Lance."

Hank writes the name on his notepad. Joyce looks at him, and they stand. They make eye contact with Rachel and wave. She looks up from her tablet, smiles, and waves back. I feel sick.

How could I not help? How could I turn my back on my niece and sister in their time of need?

Grace walks behind the detectives as they descend the stairs and open the front door. Hank walks out, but Joyce turns back to Grace.

"Do you ever iron?" she asks.

Grace frowns in surprise. "Yes, when needed."

"Do you use starch when you iron?"

Grace shrugs. "I mean, I have starch. I guess, sometimes. When it's warranted."

Joyce nods and extends her hand. "Thank you for your time."

Chapter 20

After leaving Grace's house, the detectives head back to the office to take part in a group meeting unrelated to the case, and my mind focuses back on my family. I check the hospital and find my body alone. Nobody's visiting. I wonder about James, but I can't stop thinking about my oldest son, David. Why does he keep calling me Rita? What happened to our relationship? Why had it deteriorated so much? And is that why he's vandalizing lockers at school?

I concentrate hard and see my oldest son. He's at the Sandwich Tree, a sandwich joint only a few miles from home. He's behind the counter wearing an apron and a hat and making sandwiches. Behind the register is a pretty girl about his age. She has her hair pulled back, and she's wearing a visor. She's cute and perky with the customers and employees. He's clearly distracted by her, constantly looking in her direction. He keeps stealing glances between or while making sandwiches. After a few minutes, there's a break in the orders, and a rotund woman in her mid thirties approaches.

"I think the dinner rush is over. You two can take off now."

David nods and pulls off his apron. The girl does the same, but it catches on her ponytail. David notices and looks at her awkwardly. The manager looks at David and motions, mouthing, "Help her."

David looks startled and then blurts out, "Hey, do you need some help?"

The girl looks at him; the apron stuck in the back of the visor just over her ponytail. "Thanks," she says.

She turns her back to him, dropping her hands, and David fumbles with the back, freeing the apron. She turns around, and he hands it to her.

"Thank you," she says.

"No problem."

The manager says, "Hey, we've got some extra brownies that will just go to waste. Do you guys want them?"

David looks at her, then at the girl.

The girl smiles. "Want to share some?"

David's cheeks color and all he can do is nod. The manager smiles and tells them to go sit in one of the empty booths. She'll bring them over.

David walks to the booth and sits down first, followed by the girl. They look at each other, and David's cheeks color again.

"I didn't think you'd work today," the girl says.

"Why?"

"Your mom..."

"Oh, yeah. Well..."

The manager comes over and gives them the brownies and then walks away, smiling. David pulls off a chunk of brownie and pops it in his mouth. The girl takes a small piece but only holds it in her hand.

"Is it as bad as they say on TV?"

David shrugs, reaching for more brownies. "What do they say on TV?"

The girl pauses, clearly not wanting to say. Finally, she takes a bite of the brownie and covers her mouth. "They say it's serious. That she's in a coma."

"Yeah," David says, stuffing more brownies in his mouth. At this rate, it'll be gone in seconds. He's eaten three-quarters of it already.

"I'm sorry."

David shrugs. "It's not like I saw her very much, anyway."

"What do you mean? Did she travel all the time?"

"Not really. She was just never home. She was always working. Even when she was home, she was taking calls or responding to emails, always on her phone. She's not a wonderful mom. You know?"

The girl nods, the ponytail swishing along her shoulders. "Was she always like that?"

David shakes his head. He reaches for more brownies, then stops himself. "When I was little, she was a great mom. She was always home. She helped in the school, made dinner, all that stuff. My dad worked, and she stayed home with me and my brothers. But then she started BEAU, and it went better than anyone imagined. She was working all the time. It's all she cared about. She didn't care about us anymore." He shrugs. "At first it was okay. She was still home. But the last few years, after the New York City firm invested in it, she opened an office, and I only saw her in the morning before school."

"She wouldn't come home?"

"Just sometimes. But it was late. Even on the weekends, she was working. I don't even know the last time I talked to her." David frowns and looks down. "I miss her. I think I'm the only one that remembers how she used to be. Maybe Donovan. My little brothers don't. They're used to my dad doing everything. I feel bad for him."

The girl reaches across the table and pats his hand. He looks down at her hand on his, then up into her eyes.

"I don't even know if I should say this," David says.

"What?"

He shakes his head. "The thing is, she changed. Even when she was around, she wasn't fun. Everything we did was wrong. It was better when she wasn't home. Whenever she was, she was always yelling. Never happy. Never satisfied. Reminding us all what she does for the family. She'd always point out our cars and house and say none of that would be around if not for her." He chuckles. "I mean, yeah, that's true. But it's not like life was better. Our old house was fine. We were happy."

"Hey, we're going to lock up now." The manager calls out to them from behind the counter.

David nods, and they stand from the booth. The girl turns and walks slowly toward the door, clearly wanting to stay with him.

"David, could you take the garbage on the way out?" the manager says.

"Sure," he says, and the manager hands it to him.

The girl holds the door as David slips by and heads for the dumpster.

"Hey, if you ever want to talk, you can call me," she says.

David turns around, the garbage bag slung over his shoulder. "Yeah?"

She smiles and ducks her head. "Yeah. What's your number? I'll text you, so you have mine."

He recites his digits as she taps them into her phone.

"Sent," she says.

"Cool."

They stand awkwardly, looking at each other.

"Okay, well, I gotta go," she says.

"Yeah."

They wave to each other, and she gets in an old, black Toyota Corolla and pulls away.

After tossing the trash in the dumpster, David walks over to his Toyota Camry, passing a silver Dodge Charger I know well. When he does, the detectives exit the car.

"David Burch?"

He stops, looking up at the large black man and the small white woman.

"Can we talk to you for a minute?"

"Uh..." He edges toward the car.

"We're detectives with the Idaho Falls Police Department. Do you know anything about smashed lockers at Skyline High School?"

They can't be serious. They know what he's going through, and they're going to bully him about the lockers?

David stops swaying and holds still. He darts a glance at the Camry.

Joyce steps closer. "You might not recognize us, but we're investigating your mom's fall at your house. We went to the school today and learned you've been smashing up lockers."

David puts his hand to his cheek and tries to talk, but Joyce raises her hand to stop him.

"We're the only ones who know, and it'll stay that way as long as you promise to stop."

David's breathing rapidly and looks from Joyce to Hank.

Hank nods. "Do you promise?"

"Yes."

"I want to hear you say it," Joyce says.

"I promise."

"Good. Now we want to know something about your brother."

"Donovan?"

"Yes. Where's he going instead of school?"

David shakes his head. "What do you mean?"

"He's leaving school every day. He hasn't been in three weeks. Where's he going?"

David shrugs. "I don't know."

"You don't know where he's going, or you don't want to tell us?"

David looks from Joyce to Hank and back. "I don't know where he's going. I know he's not going to class. I just don't know where."

Joyce purses her lips. "Why's he missing class?"

"I don't know. He won't say. I heard someone might be bullying him."

Chapter 21

The thing about being in a coma is your body is sleeping all the time. I don't know how it works for others. Maybe I'm a one-in-a-billion case, but I'm conscious and aware of everything, even though it doesn't show. That's good and bad. Good, because I know what's going on. Bad, because I'm awake all night with nothing to do. I can't even turn on a TV or pick up a phone. I can't read a book. Everyone I know is asleep, and I'm bored. I'm left alone with my thoughts.

Having no physical body leaves me completely dependent on others. I live through them with no memory of myself. I learn about myself through them, and when they aren't active, I'm not active. In times like this, I'm most comfortable around my body. I linger in the room, hoping that something will change.

As I look at my body, I'm disgusted. I hate the person I've become. Whether it's neighbors, coworkers, or family. Everyone agrees. I'm a terrible person. I'm myopic, only caring for myself. I'm unforgiving, critical, greedy. No wonder I'm alone. Maybe my father is right. James should shut off the machines.

The intensive-care floor of the hospital quiets down at night. The lights are dimmed, and visiting hours are over. I'm still connected to a ventilator, and monitors measure brain movement and heart rate. The door opens, and Ginger, my nurse, enters with a man I don't recognize. He's wearing scrubs, and I assume he's another nurse.

"Do you mind helping me turn her?" Ginger says to the man. "I'm afraid she's going to get bedsores, and I'm not sure how long she'll go on."

The man walks to the other side of the bed. "What happened to her? She looks young."

"Yeah, she's only forty-one. It's really sad. She fell off her balcony. Her husband found her."

"Is this Rita Burch?"

Ginger nods. They're standing over my body on either end of the bed.

"I heard about her on TV. She's the founder of BEAU. The richest woman in the state."

Ginger sighs. "Not for much longer. Her husband's going to be."

"Not going to make it, huh?"

Ginger shakes her head. "The doctors don't think so. They're going to talk to the husband again tomorrow. Encourage him to pull the plug."

"She's got kids, right?"

"Four."

"Wow."

Ginger points to my side. "I don't want to move her much. She has multiple broken bones and a subdural hematoma. We've got to be gentle but, on the off chance she makes it, I don't want to add bedsores to the pain she'll experience."

Working together, they turn my body just enough to satisfy Ginger. She thanks him, checks to make sure everything works correctly, and exits, pulling the door shut behind her.

Again, I'm alone, looking at my broken body. Before, I just had swelling. Now I see dark shadows around my eyes, forehead, and limbs. Ginger says that the doctors are going to encourage James to turn off the machines. Everyone's giving up.

I concentrate my mind and find James. He's lying in bed. The TV's on. He stays on one side: the other side is empty. He's saving it for me. I look at Reed and Gilbert, my babies, asleep in their beds, unaware they may say goodbye to their mom tomorrow. I wonder, do they even miss me? I was so caught up in work for so long. Has their world changed? If I die, will it matter to them? They'll miss me, right? Or will James move on? Will he have all the money and find a new woman? Is that what he wants? My heart hurts at the thought of another woman raising my babies, and I have to turn away.

I move downstairs into David's room. It's a mess. He's lying in bed watching videos on his phone. He smiles at a video of "fails." The smile masks the struggles he's facing. Did I know? Did I ever ask?

Finally, I check on Donovan. I don't find him in bed. I check the couch, and he isn't there. I find him in the bathroom. He's sitting on the toilet, fully clothed, tears streaming down his face. His heart is breaking. His glasses are fogging up, and he takes them off and places them on the sink. The image disturbs me. What's making him so sad? Is it school? Is it me?

He stays on the toilet sobbing as my heart melts. I want so badly to wake up and hold him. Help him. After five minutes, he stops and stands. He exits the bathroom and climbs into bed. He stares at the wall, and I wonder what's happening in his head.

Chapter 22

After staying with Donovan until he fell asleep, I returned to the hospital and waited until morning. Yesterday, as Hank and Joyce parted, they discussed a meeting scheduled for eight. I channel Joyce and see her exiting her vehicle in the back of the building behind the alarmed fence. She enters the building and gets a cup of coffee, then sits at her desk checking email. Hank walks in a few minutes later. It's five to eight when she looks up and sees him.

"I'll meet you in the conference room."

Hank nods.

Joyce carries her laptop, coffee, notepad, and pen. The room is set with an overhead projector and three tables with chairs arranged in a *U*. She takes a seat next to the projector and plugs it into her laptop. A woman I've seen walking around the office comes in next. She's holding an open laptop in one hand and a notepad in the other. They greet each other. Joyce calls her Sarah, and I recognize the name. Joyce has talked to her several times on the phone. She's an assistant in the investigation.

Hank enters next. He carries a laptop and notepad, just like Sarah. He has bags under his eyes and slumps in a chair. He takes a position near Joyce on the other side of the projector.

A young man, maybe a year or two younger than Hank, enters next. He sits beside Sarah. He's followed by Captain Rigby. Everyone but the captain has their laptop open and a notepad and pen. The captain carries only a notepad. He sits by himself at the table closest to the door. Joyce waits for a signal from the captain to begin the meeting. He nods to her.

"Good morning, everyone," she says.

They all mumble good mornings in return.

"The purpose of this meeting is to run down the status of the case regarding Rita Burch. As you all know, after finding forensic evidence at the scene of the accident, the fall was deemed to be intentional. We believe someone tried to kill her. First by making her slip, hoping she'd fall from the balcony. When that failed, they pushed her. We know this for several reasons, primarily by the location of the impact of her body on the patio below."

Joyce looks at Hank. "Since beginning the investigation, Hank and I feel more strongly than ever that someone did, in fact, try to kill her. Our job is to find out who and why." She pauses and looks at everyone. "You all know how high profile this case is. It's important that we do it right."

They all nod, and Joyce turns on the projector. "We thought it'd be helpful to review our notes on the case, beginning with the most likely suspects."

Just what I've been waiting for.

A photo of James lights up the screen.

"As you all know, this is James Burch, Rita's husband. He has the most to gain, and an argument can be made, the most to lose with Rita's death. He would inherit everything—the business and all assets. The only problem, the value of the business would drop significantly if Rita were to die. Hank and I believe he's likely not the killer; however, he had an opportunity. After dropping the kids off at school, he could have come back, thrown her off the balcony, then called nine-one-one. Because of this, we can't yet eliminate him as a suspect."

"Why don't you think he's the killer?" the captain asks. "You said he has the most to gain and motive."

Joyce looks at Hank, then back to the captain. "I misspoke. One of us thinks he's the killer, one of us doesn't."

The captain looks between Joyce and Hank. "Hank thinks he's the killer, but you don't."

"Correct," Joyce says.

"So, why don't you, Joyce?"

"Other than a weak motive, nothing about him speaks to a violent nature. He's never raised a hand to Rita or the boys. Nothing in his nature says violence."

"That we know of," Hank says.

"Yes, that we know of."

"But wouldn't you say this is an unusual case?" the captain asks.

"Certainly," Joyce says.

"How were they getting along?"

"There was friction in the home," Hank says.

"But not violent," the captain says.

"No. At least nothing documented."

The captain nods. "What were they fighting about?"

"Mostly Rita's absence. Her focus on work," Hank says.

The captain starts to speak, but Joyce cuts him off. "We're not eliminating him as a suspect. We're just giving a status update. He's still very much on our list."

The captain nods and turns back to the screen. Joyce moves on.

The next image is of David.

"This is David Burch, Rita's oldest son. He's seventeen years old and was listed as present in his geography class at the time of the accident. It's possible that he left during the class and came back, although unlikely. Nobody in the class remembers him leaving. Because of this, we don't think he's our killer; however, he's angry and can be violent. He has a temper and isn't happy with his mother. For the last year, he's been calling her by her first name. He's bitter about the time she spends away from the family. He's struggling in school."

Joyce looks over at Hank, but he says nothing, and she moves on.

"Next is Donovan Burch. He's sixteen, and Rita's second-oldest son. He's high on our suspect list. He was marked absent in his math class at the time of the accident, and neither the teacher nor his fellow students remember seeing him. That's nothing new because he hasn't attended a single class for the last two weeks. We aren't sure where he's going or why, but that's top on our priority list for today."

"You think it's him," Captain Rigby says.

Joyce bobbles her head from side to side. "It could be. Something isn't right about him."

"What's his motive?" Captain Rigby asks.

"The day of the accident, James took the boys in to see their mother. Donovan wouldn't go. Although not nearly as demonstrative in his anger, we think Donovan harbors bitter feelings for her. The counselor at the high school says Donovan is shy and reserved around other kids. There have been reports of him being bullied. We think he might have turned his frustration on the person he blamed most."

Joyce looks around the room, but nobody responds, so she moves on.

"Next, we have Steve Anderson. Steve is Rita's estranged father. Rita hasn't spoken to him in eight years. He cheated on her mother and left her, and not long after, her mother died from a heart attack. She blamed him for what happened and never forgave him. Around the same time, Steve lost his job in pharmaceutical sales. He's been scraping by as a sales associate at a car dealership. He has poor financial acumen and is severely in debt." Joyce takes a big breath. "Over the last few years, since Rita's business took off, he's reached out asking her for money. Every time she's ignored him; however," Joyce raises her index finger, "for the last year, Steve has received anonymous deposits into his account. We believe James has been giving him money, unbeknownst to Rita. Steve pretty well confirmed it. His motive is obvious—he needs money and sees James as the person to help him. With Rita out of the way, his prospects improve. He also has no alibi for the time of the accident. He claims to be home alone."

"One problem," Hank says.

"What's that?" the captain asks.

"Why now? If he had waited a couple more weeks, James would have been so rich that he could have given him ten million without blinking an eye. Steve claims he didn't know that. But we wonder."

Sarah raises a hand, and Joyce points to her. "Also, the news of BEAU going public wasn't a secret. It was all over the internet. If Steve was paying any kind of attention, he would have seen it."

Joyce nods. "That's true; however, Steve doesn't strike me as the sharpest knife in the drawer. He could have made a big mistake."

They all nod, and Joyce moves on.

"Next is Erin Callahan, Rita's assistant at BEAU. She's technically an employee of Symbiotic, not BEAU, the private equity firm that invested in BEAU. She despises Rita and isn't shy about it. A year ago, she called her boss at Symbiotic and begged to leave BEAU and return to New York. He wouldn't let her."

"But wouldn't she be released from the position after it went public? Wouldn't she go back to New York?" asks the captain.

"Yes," Joyce says, "but perhaps she thought she could get hold of the company."

"How?"

"We aren't sure yet."

"Does she have an alibi?"

"Yes, but it's shaky."

"How so?"

"She claims to have been on the Zoom call Rita scheduled that morning, but we don't know if that's true. The call never started because Rita was the organizer and never began the meeting. Plus, she could have logged in from a phone, so she could have been anywhere."

"Hmm," Captain Rigby says.

"Next is Grace, Rita's sister. Like her father, Rita hasn't talked to her in years. They had a falling out over Steve. Grace wanted Rita to forgive, but Rita wouldn't. It got heated. Since then, they haven't talked."

Hank jumps in. "It was more Grace not wanting to talk to Rita, in this case."

"Right," Joyce says. "She's married and has two kids of her own. She seems happy. Her husband's a schoolteacher. She works part-time in a café. They're getting by. They have little money but differ from Steve because they don't ask for any."

"So why is she a suspect?" the captain asks.

Joyce and Hank look at each other. "Without anything concrete, we've been reluctant to remove anyone from the list."

"I'd put her at a low priority," the captain says.

"Agreed," Hank and Joyce say in unison.

"Finally, we have her neighbors," Joyce says.

"Plural?" the captain asks.

"Yes, but one in particular."

A photo of Kim comes up on the screen.

"Kim Long. She's going through a divorce. Her husband is a doctor. Two kids. Her youngest plays on the basketball team with

Rita's youngest. She lives three houses down from the Burches. She's friends with Rita. They work out together. She brought the boys to the hospital after the accident. She was also the first to visit the hospital."

"What's her motive?"

Hank shrugs, and Joyce looks at him, then nods. "We aren't sure. We feel we shouldn't eliminate her yet. She doesn't have a solid alibi; however, she was getting the kids off to school and even ran her daughter to school that morning. We were able to confirm that. James drove her oldest in the carpool. It's possible she could have done it, but it would have been difficult. She had to be to work at nine."

"How'd she come to the hospital then? How'd she know?"

"One of the other neighbors called. They asked if she knew anything. She left work to go over."

"Hmm, seems like another low priority."

Joyce nods and looks at Hank.

The young guy, who hasn't spoken, raises his hand. He's been tapping his foot nervously throughout the meeting. The captain nods at him.

"Whatcha got, Trevor?"

"I think you need to add one other name to your suspect list."

Joyce and Hank frown.

"I've been analyzing the data from Rita's phone. She was having an affair."

"What?" the captain asks, slapping the table. "You had this the whole time and said nothing?"

Trevor ducks his red face and holds up a hand. "I just found it. And she just broke it off with him the day before."

"Who?" Hank and Joyce ask in unison.

"Robert Love, the contractor who built the Burch home."

Chapter 23

After the bombshell Trevor had dropped in the meeting, I stayed with the detectives. Joyce called Robert Love, my contractor, and apparent secret lover, and set a meeting. Last night, as I watched myself sleep, I hated the figure in front of me. That hate has become loathing. For the first time, I think Kim might be right. I could see why I would want to kill myself. I don't deserve to live. If someone did try to kill me, I wish they'd succeeded. If I could, I'd pull the plug myself.

Now I watch as Hank and Joyce follow the host to a booth near the back of the restaurant. They sit opposite each other, and the host hands them menus and asks for a drink order. Joyce requests a Diet Coke while Hank gets water. When she's gone, Joyce says, "Would you rather sit at a table?"

Even though the booths are large, a man of Hank's size has difficulty squeezing in. Even with his back against the rest, his stomach pushes against the table.

"It's fine," he says, sliding his tie away from the table. It had been crammed between the table and his stomach.

"What happens when he gets here?" Joyce asks.

"What do you mean?"

"You're sitting over there. You want him to sit next to me?"

Hank hadn't thought of that.

"Should I come over there?"

Joyce shakes her head and slides to the end of the booth, standing. "Come on." She walks across the restaurant and picks a square table with four chairs. She sits down and looks up at Hank.

"Shouldn't we ask?"

"Are they going to say no?"

Hank considers that and then sits down in the chair next to her.

Joyce selected a chair facing the restaurant and the booth they had come from. After a minute, a server comes around the corner, holding a tray of drinks. She looks at the booth, stops, and then looks around the restaurant. Joyce holds up a hand. The girl waves and comes over.

"A booth wasn't going to work for us. I'm the Diet Coke."

"Oh, no problem." The girl gives her the Diet Coke and puts a large glass of water in front of Hank. "And you're waiting for one more?"

"Yes," Joyce tells her.

The girl smiles and puts another water opposite Joyce.

"I'll come back and check on you in a few minutes."

"Thanks," Joyce says, and the server leaves.

"So, how do you want to play this?" Hank asks, gulping water.

Joyce takes the straw from the paper wrapper and puts it in her Diet Coke. "Why don't you start? Stay casual. See what he knows. I'll jump in once I have a sense of him."

Hank nods, and the host comes around the corner with a man following behind. He's sporting a baseball cap with his company logo on it and wearing jeans and a golf shirt. The host stops when she sees the empty booth. She turns and looks at the man and says something.

"Hey," Joyce calls out.

Everyone in the room looks at her, which is only two other people at the booth along the windows. Joyce waves to the girl, and she bids the man to follow her to their table. Joyce and Hank stand. The man is in his late forties, of medium height, and has tanned, weather-worn skin, and a shadow of a beard. He's moderately attractive but no heartthrob. What was I thinking?

"Robert," Joyce says, extending a hand. "I'm Detective Joyce Powers, and this is Hank Gardener."

"Bob," he says, shaking her hand, then Hank's. They all sit down, and the host hands him a menu.

"Your server will be right with you," she says, walking away.

"Have you been here before?" Bob asks.

"Once or twice," Hank says.

"They've got good burgers," Bob says. "I recommend them."

The server comes around the corner, holding a notepad. When she reaches the table, she looks at Bob. His eyes are on the menu.

"Bob?" she says, beaming.

He looks up at her. "Oh. Hi, Crystal."

"I thought you were out of town?"

Bob steals a glance at the detectives, then looks back at her. "I just got back. Had to come back early for business."

She nods and looks at Hank and Joyce, then back at him. "You should have told me."

He takes a breath. "Yeah, sorry about that. I'll call you. Can I get an iced tea?" he says and turns away from her.

She looks at him for a moment, surprise on her face. "Sure," she says, turning her attention to Hank and Joyce. Her smile is forced. "Do you all need a minute to order?"

"No, we're ready," Joyce says, asking for a chicken salad.

Hank orders a burger, and so does Bob. Bob doesn't look at the server. The girl frowns at him and walks away.

Bob shrugs when she's out of earshot. "I went on a date with her a couple of weeks ago. I forgot she works here."

Hank nods, and Joyce says nothing.

Bob takes a drink of water, and then leans forward, putting his elbows on the table. "Listen, I just want to be clear. She demanded the height of the railing. I warned her and her husband about the risks. But," he shrugs, "the customer is always right. You know?"

"Rita wanted that railing height on the balcony?"

"Yeah...she was really particular. She wanted a specific chair and didn't want the top of the railing in her view as she sat in the chair looking out. She demanded I take six inches off the height. I told her it was against code, but she wouldn't hear it. She was going to fire me over it." He shakes his head and puts his hands on his cheeks. "I just couldn't believe my luck that she fell off."

"Your luck," Hanks says.

"Yeah, I mean, the one time I put in a railing against code, this happens."

"Pretty bad luck," Hank says.

"Tell me about it," Bob agrees.

"Worse for her," Hank says.

Bob nods and then stops, his eyes narrowing. He leans back in his chair and crosses his arms. "What's that supposed to mean? I didn't mean for that to happen to Rita."

Hank stares back at him. "What'd you do? Have the inspector come out, approve the home, then change it afterward?"

Bob frowns. "Do I need a lawyer?"

Joyce raises a hand. "Bob, we really don't care about the height of the railing. That's not why we asked you to meet us."

Bob glares at Hank, then looks at Joyce. "No?"

"No," she says.

"Why then?"

"We want to understand your relationship with Rita."

"Simple. I built her house. To tell you the truth, I couldn't wait to be done. She was very particular and demanding."

Hank looks at him and coughs and almost says something, but stops when he sees the look in Joyce's eyes.

"Did you have any interaction with Rita after the home was finished?"

Bob swallows and shakes his head. "Other than a couple of questions here and there, no."

Hank sighs and rolls his eyes. Bob looks back at him.

"What's your problem, man?"

Hank takes a swallow of water and then sets the glass down on the table. "No problem. I just don't like liars."

"I'm not lying," Bob growls.

"Then the phone records must be wrong," Hank says.

Bob starts to respond and stops. He looks at Hank, then Joyce. "There aren't any phone records."

Joyce looks at him like a parent scolding a child. "We have her phone. Maybe messaging through WhatsApp doesn't show on phone records. But there's a backup file created and stored on the phone."

A bead of perspiration appears below Bob's hat, and he wipes it away with his napkin. He takes a deep breath and leans back in his chair. "Okay, look, yeah, maybe I was seeing Rita afterward. But that ended before she fell."

Joyce waits for the server to reach their table. The girl gives Joyce her food first, then hands a burger to Hank, pauses, and gives it to Bob instead. The last plate she gives to Hank.

"Anything else I can get you right now?" she asks.

"I'm fine," Joyce says.

Bob and Hank shake their heads. She looks at Bob again, but he doesn't return her gaze, and she walks away.

Bob picks up the ketchup and dumps some on his plate.

"What do you mean, it was over before she fell?" Joyce asks.

Bob shakes his head. "She messaged me the night before. She said she had to end our relationship. That it couldn't go on any longer."

"Did she say why?" Joyce asks.

"No. She just said it was over."

Bob dunks a couple of fries into the ketchup and pops them in his mouth.

"Did that make you mad?" Hank asks.

Bob shakes his head. "No. Why should it? It's not like I was looking to marry her. I was just having fun. I went on a date the next day."

"With Crystal?" Joyce asks.

He pauses. "No, I don't think so."

"With another married woman?" Hank asks.

Bob glares at him.

"Where were you the morning of the accident?" Joyce asks.

"Tuesday morning?"

Joyce nods.

"I was at a business networking meeting."

"Where?"

"At the Shilo Inn. We meet once a week on Tuesdays."

"Can anyone else verify that?" Hank asks.

"Yeah, like twenty other local business owners. Look, do I need a lawyer?"

"Is there one in the group?" Hank asks.

"You're a real jerk, you know that?" Bob says, raising his voice and coming forward in his chair.

Hank smiles.

"Do you like to iron?" Joyce asks before taking a bite of her salad.

He stops and looks at her. "What?"

"Clothes. Do you like to iron clothes? An entrepreneur like you. You must have occasion to iron your clothes."

Bob glares at her. "What are you talking about?"

She meets his gaze, then shrugs. "Just curious. Do you?"

"No."

"You never iron?"

"I mean, I have."

"Do you own an iron?"

"Yes."

"What about starch? Do you starch your shirts?"

"Are you serious?"

Joyce shrugs. "Seems like a straightforward question to answer."

He shakes his head. "No. I take my shirts to a dry cleaner."

"But you said you have an iron?"

"Yes, I have one. And yes, I've used it before. But I don't even remember the last time."

"Okay," Joyce says.

Chapter 24

After Joyce pays the bill, I watch as the detectives walk out of the restaurant and get into the Charger, leaving Bob engaged in a heated phone conversation with one of his subcontractors.

"Nice job in there, Hank," Joyce says.

Hank puts the car in reverse and pulls out of the parking space. Joyce watches the people filling in and out of the restaurant.

"He made it easy. What a douchebag."

Hank pulls out onto the street. After a minute of silence, he says, "I'm not like him, am I? You don't see me that way, do you?"

Joyce looks away from the window. "What do you mean?"

Hank gives her a knowing look.

Joyce shakes her head. "Not unless the woman you cheated with was in a committed relationship as well." Joyce looks away from him. "Was she?"

Hank shakes his head.

Joyce looks at him, then back out the window. "Has it happened again?"

Hank looks at her. "Never."

Joyce points out the window. "Pull over. Right there along the curb."

Hank gives her a quizzical look but follows her command and eases the car over. When the vehicle stops, Joyce watches him and then looks out at the park.

"Do you know what park this is?"

"Freeman?"

Joyce nods, still looking out the window, her mind somewhere else. "Do you know anything about the history? What this park was before?"

Hank frowns and shakes his head.

"It was a landfill. A garbage dump."

I can tell Hank has the same thought as me. How? Not a trace of trash can be seen anywhere among the beautiful trees and grass.

"It's beautiful, right?"

"Yes," Hank agrees.

"Seeing it now, nobody would ever guess there're thousands of tons of garbage below us." Now she turns and looks Hank in the eye. "My own trash is buried here. Probably tons of it. What do you think people would say if I grabbed a shovel and started digging for it?"

Hank smiles. "It'd confirm what people say about you."

She rolls her eyes. "Hank, just like my trash, your mistake is better left buried. There's no good that comes from bringing it up. Leave it where it is and move on. Forgive yourself." She pauses and stares into his eyes until she's sure he's heard her. "No, you're nothing like Bob Love. The fact that you asked proves it. You made a mistake, confessed, and haven't done it since. That's completely different from ole Bobby there." She sighs. "Okay?"

Hank swallows and nods.

Joyce winks and looks away from him. "The question is...what to do about it?"

Hank looks at the large pine tree towering above them. "James?"

Joyce nods. "Do you think he knew?"

Hank pulls away from the curb and pulls back onto the road. After several seconds, he shakes his head. "I don't think so. We could ask him?"

Joyce closes her eyes and rubs her forehead. "We could, but then we're telling a married man about an affair his wife had while she lays in bed dying." She sighs. "I don't know about you, but I'd just as soon avoid it if we could."

"You know the danger there."

"Oh, I know. If he knew, that's motive." Neither speaks as they consider the implications.

"What was your take on Bobby the ladies' man? Do you think he's good for it?"

Joyce shakes her head. "Nah. Unfortunately, it wouldn't make sense."

"How so?"

"First, I believe what he said. I don't think she was anything more than another conquest. He's already back in the game. Heck, he was already *still* in the game. He dated Crystal during the affair. Second, he doesn't strike me as all that bright, but even he wouldn't make that big a mistake. Speaking of which," she smiles, "do you think that server spit in his burger?"

Hank laughs. "Absolutely. The way she made sure I got one burger, and he got the other." He chuckles. "But I don't follow. What mistake?"

She grins, then looks back out the window. "Why would the man who broke the law by installing a railing against code draw attention to the fact?"

Hank takes his eyes off the road, a dumbfounded expression on his face. She looks back at him and winks.

"Maybe it was a crime of passion? She broke up with him the day before, and he wanted revenge. He knew the railing was low, so it could be perceived as an accident," Hank says.

She grimaces and shakes her head. "You're giving him too much credit. The crime-of-passion part I could maybe see. Except, I really believe she was nothing to him but the latest piece of tail. I saw no sign that he worried about her well-being. She's laying in a hospital bed fighting for her life, and he never asked after her once. Yes, he knew about the railing height. But the smart criminal would push her off, knowing it would implicate him in a lower crime to cover the bigger one." She clicks her tongue. "Bobby isn't that clever." She stops and puts up a finger. "However, I think he still has a part to play in all this. I'm just not sure what it is yet." Joyce looks down at her watch. "Let's head back to the office. I've got to meet Sam in a half hour."

"Boise trip tonight?"

She nods.

Chapter 25

I leave the detectives and return to my hospital room. Although I'm gaining so much knowledge about myself by following them, I don't enjoy being away from my body for long. What if something happens? What if James does something or my body gives out? Will my consciousness just disappear? I guess it doesn't matter. I want to die. Even so, it's hard to let go.

When my consciousness returns to the hospital room, I find James alone, seated in a chair across from the bed. He's several feet from my body, but his eyes aren't on me. He's looking at his phone. I hover over him, curious about what has his attention. I'm not sure what I expected to see, but it wasn't this.

He's looking at photos. Pictures of me. Images of us in different places. Some with our boys, some just the two of us. He stops on one and smiles. It's a photo of me. He must be the one behind the camera. I'm standing in a bedroom. Small flecks of paint cover my face, hands, and hair. I hold a paint roller. I'm looking at him and laughing. I'm young, no more than twenty-five. My stomach is enormous. I look like I'm ready to deliver a baby any day. Happiness gleams through my eyes.

He looks up from his phone and focuses on my physical shape. The smile disappears, and his eyes droop. In an instant, his face morphs from joy to sorrow. His eyes fall back to his phone, and he swipes with his finger.

His smile returns. He swipes several times and stops. It's a photo of us. We're standing over a wedding cake. I'm wearing a simple but lovely white gown, and he's in a dark tuxedo. My hand is extended, pushing cake into his face. He swipes again. The next image is of us kissing. The cake covers his face, and he's pressing it into mine while I laugh. He startles me as he chuckles, looking at the photo.

He swipes again, and he's holding me to him. We stand in the middle of a dance floor. All the wedding guests surround us as we look into each other's eyes. My husband sits, staring at the photo, when a tear rolls down his cheek and drops onto the phone. One tear becomes many as sobs rack his body. His heart is breaking right in front of me, and all I can do is watch as a wave of guilt overcomes me. At this moment, I realize how much he loves me. He longs for what we had. What I used to be.

I wonder, does he know? Did he find out?

I was a cheater. Just like my father. The hypocrisy is almost comical. I couldn't forgive my father for what he did and then turned around and did the very same thing. Watching James fall apart, I realize something. Even though I neglected him, even though I took him for granted, he still loves me. If that's true, how could he kill me?

He takes several quick breaths, and the sobbing stops. He stands and walks over to a tissue box and wipes his nose and eyes. He looks at me with swollen eyes and takes several steps closer. He looks down at me, then hesitates. He looks as if he wants to say something but can't find the words.

The door opens. Dr. Mitchell stands in the doorframe along with another woman in a white doctor's uniform. I've never seen the second woman before. Dr. Mitchell looks at James, then at my body, and enters, followed by the other doctor.

"How is she?" Dr. Mitchell asks.

"No change," James says.

Dr. Mitchell approaches and looks at me. She touches my hand, then leans over my face and opens one eye. She shines a light into the lifeless eyes, scrutinizing them, then steps back. She looks up at James.

"Can we talk for a minute?"

James nods, and she motions to the chair he typically sits in.

After he's seated, the doctors pull two chairs around so they form a triangle.

"James, this is Dr. Nora Saunders. Dr. Saunders is a therapist who specializes in supporting families who've experienced trauma. I've asked her to be present today because I have a serious matter to discuss with you."

James looks at her and nods. She gives him a supportive smile.

Dr. Mitchell sighs. "James, this morning, we did another round of tests on Rita. I'm sorry to say, the results were the same. We see no evidence of brain function. If not for the machines, she wouldn't be breathing on her own. We hoped that, by now, we'd see some progress. Something would change. But..." she shakes her head, "I'm afraid the chances that something would change now are nearly zero."

Tears well up again in James's eyes.

Dr. Saunders offers him the tissue box, and he takes one and dabs at his eyes.

Dr. Mitchell frowns. "James, I'm afraid it's time to consider turning off the machines."

Tears flow more freely. After several seconds, James composes himself. "When?"

Dr. Mitchell looks at Dr. Saunders, then back at him. "That's up to you. If you decide it's time, it's fairly simple on our end. For you, consider who you'd like to have in the room. You can have as few or as many people as you like, though I'd recommend not exceeding ten."

"Is she feeling any pain?"

Dr. Mitchell shakes her head. "We don't think so. Her brain function is nonexistent. When we turn the machines off, she'll go pretty quickly. Some people linger, but given her brain function, I think she'd pass within seconds. Minutes, at most. She won't feel anything."

James nods. "Do I need to decide now?"

"No, not at all. You can take the night to consider it. We can check back in the morning."

James nods, and she reaches forward and pats his hand. Both doctors stand, re-situate the chairs, and leave, shutting the door behind them. James sits, not moving, and I can't stop wondering what he was going to say.

Chapter 26

After a long night of being alone with my thoughts, I'm eager to once again follow the detectives. Yesterday, after learning about the affair, I'd given up on myself. I wanted to die. I was convinced that everyone would be better off without me. I was like George Bailey in *It's a Wonderful Life*. I believed the world would be better without me. But then I watched James. I saw the love in his eyes as he flipped through the photos on the phone. For the first time since waking after my accident, I felt loved.

At 7:35 a.m., I find the detectives sitting in the car down the street from my home. From their conversation, I know they're waiting for David and Donovan. But the boys still haven't emerged from the house.

"Maybe they're not going today?" Hank says.

Joyce says nothing. After a minute, she asks, "Who sings this song?"

Hank shakes his head. "Of course, you'd ask on this one. I knew the last three before now."

Joyce shrugs. "So you say. Plus, not my problem."

Hank turns up the music.

The world I love, the tears I drop
To be part of the wave, can't stop
Ever wonder if it's all for you?
The world I love, the trains I hop
To be part of the wave, can't stop
Come and tell me when it's time to

"Goo Goo Dolls?" he asks, frowning.

Joyce grimaces.

He pauses. "Wait, do they sing 'Californication?'"

There's disappointment in her eyes. "Who sings it, though? What's the band?"

"Oh, come on," he says. "Give me some credit."

"Nope. I need the band."

He rubs his chin and growls. "Pearl Jam."

She shakes her head. "Nice try."

He smacks the steering wheel, then stops and looks up. David and Donovan have emerged from the house. They pile into the old Camry and pull away from the curb, not bothering to signal. The detectives roll behind them. The high school is only a five-minute drive from the house, and when they reach it, they pull into the parking lot. Although they're fifteen minutes after the bell, they walk to the school like they have nowhere they need to be.

Hank and Joyce watch from the parking lot as they enter the building.

"Maybe he's actually going today," Hank says.

But, almost on cue, Donovan reemerges from the school. He crosses the parking lot and gets back into the car. He pulls out, and Hank follows.

"I guess they both have a set of keys," Hank says.

Donovan drives for several minutes and stops at the community park. He gets out of the car and walks to a nearby bench, rummages in his backpack, then pulls out a Nintendo Switch. For the next hour, he sits, doing nothing but playing a video game as the detectives watch. The time goes by so slowly, and I wonder why they don't do something. Finally, his leg bounces up and down, and he looks like he needs to pee. He goes back to the car, drives several blocks, and stops in front of an arcade called Ka-Ko-Jo's. He gets out of the car and walks into the building. The detectives follow.

When they enter through the front doors, they pause, blinking rapidly. I hadn't noticed before, but my vision adjusts perfectly, no matter where I am. I guess that's the benefit of not having physical eyes.

The detectives scan the room. The place is empty, other than an employee working behind the desk. The guy has short, brown hair and wears a black T-shirt with Mario Brothers characters all over it. He gives them a curious look. Joyce scans the place, probably looking for Donovan, then approaches the man. She shows him her badge and his eyes go wide.

"Did a boy just walk in here?"

He nods. "Donovan?"

"Yeah."

"Yeah, he went to the bathroom." His eyes narrow, and he extends a hand, palm forward, taking a step back. "Hey, am I going to be in trouble?"

Hank and Joyce just watch him.

"He doesn't come every day. I know he should be in school, but...the kid's had it rough. You know?"

"How often does he come?"

"Not every day. Maybe two or three days a week."

"Only on weekdays?"

He nods.

"Sounds like almost every day," Joyce says. "Was he here last Tuesday?"

"Maybe. I don't really remember. Mornings are slow."

A sound behind them brings their eyes around. Donovan emerges from the bathroom, sees them at the ticket counter, and bolts for the exit. Hank takes three giant steps and cuts him off. Donovan tries to run through him, but he's got a better chance with a cinderblock wall. He falls back, and Hank grabs him by the shoulders. He holds him, and Joyce turns back to the guy behind the counter.

"No more letting kids skip school to hang out here. Got it?"

The guy nods, fear in his eyes.

Hank pulls Donovan to the doors. He tries to resist, but Hank could probably pick him up by the shoulders and carry him if he wanted. "Don't make me put handcuffs on you."

When they get outside, Hank pulls Donovan to the Charger and puts him in the back seat. He flips the child locks, and Hank and Joyce get in the front.

"Put on your seat belt," Joyce says, turning around and watching him. Donovan ignores her, looking down. "Have you ever worn handcuffs?" Donovan looks up but doesn't speak. "Put on your seat belt, or the handcuffs are going on. We'll pin your arms behind your back. At first, it won't be bad; it'll only be uncomfortable. But after a minute or so, blood will drain from your arms. The cuffs will start to dig into your wrists, your shoulders will begin to ache. No matter your position, you won't be comfortable and it will only get worse. It's like having both arms go to sleep."

Donovan reaches up and grabs the belt, snapping it into place. He doesn't look at Joyce.

Hank watches him from the rearview mirror, then pulls out and onto the road.

"You've been missing a lot of class," Joyce says.

Donovan doesn't respond.

"We checked with the citizenship office. You weren't in class the morning your mom fell." Joyce turns around and looks at him. "Were you at home?"

Donovan looks at her, his lower lip trembling. His eyes become moist behind the glasses.

"Were you there?"

Donovan watches her but doesn't answer.

"Did you push your mom?"

Donovan doesn't reply.

"Did you?"

"No," Donovan whispers, looking down.

Joyce watches him closely. "Someone saw a figure running away from the house. Was that you?"

Donovan's head snaps up.

"I'm going to take that as a yes. Why were you running away from the house?"

Donovan looks down and mumbles. It's so soft that Joyce stops him. "I can't hear you."

He looks up, tears streaming down his face. "I came home. Sometimes I do that instead of going to school. I hide in my bedroom. I told David I wasn't feeling good. He wouldn't take me back to the house, so I walked. I came in through the back. When I got close..." He stops, and the tears come harder.

"She was on the patio?"

He nods and wipes his nose with his hand. Joyce looks around and finds a napkin and hands it to him.

"Then what did you do?"

"I got scared and ran."

"What direction?"

"The front."

Joyce nods. "Did you see anyone?"

He frowns. "Like who?"

"Anyone up on the balcony? Anyone in the house?"

"I didn't look in the house."

"What about the balcony?"

He hesitates.

"Did you see your dad?"

"I don't think so."

"Are you sure?"

"No, but I don't think it was him."

"Who then?"

"I don't know."

"But you saw someone?"

"I think so."

"You're not sure?"

He shakes his head. "They were in the shadows. Against the house. I was so scared I ran."

"Did you see what they were wearing? Anything about them?"

He looks back down and shakes his head. "They were dark."

"Dark? Like black?"

"No, dark clothes."

"Man or woman?"

"I don't know."

"If you had to guess."

"Woman."

"What about in the front? Did you see anyone? Were there any cars?"

"I don't know. I don't think so."

Joyce and Hank exchange a look, then she looks back at Donovan. "Then where did you go?"

"I ran down the street but stopped. I got scared, thinking maybe I left my mom. That maybe it was an accident, and she needed help and I ran away from her."

"So, what did you do?"

"I went back the same way, to the back of the house."

"Was your mom still there?"

"Yeah, but my dad was there too. He was talking on the phone. I couldn't hear what he was saying. After a few minutes, I heard sirens, and the ambulance came."

"You didn't see your dad come home?"

Donovan shakes his head.

"What was your dad wearing?"

He looks up at her.

"A black hoodie?"

"It wasn't him," Donovan says.

"The person on the balcony before? You're sure."

He looks away.

"Was it him?"

"I don't know. I don't think so. It couldn't be."

Joyce eyes him. "When you were running down the street, did you see your dad's car?"

He shakes his head.

Joyce sighs. They've pulled into the school parking lot, and Hank finds a parking space in the front. They sit for several minutes.

Finally, Joyce asks, "Why aren't you going to class?"

Donovan looks down.

"Are you getting bullied?"

Donovan looks up, then out the window at the building.

"Is it more than one kid? Or just one?"

"One," he mumbles.

"What's his name?"

Donovan doesn't answer.

"He won't know you told."

Donovan shakes his head.

Both detectives look at each other. Joyce turns back around and looks out the windshield.

After a minute, Donovan says, "Did that person on the balcony push my mom?"

Joyce doesn't look at him. "Yes."

Hank watches him in the rearview mirror.

"Do you know who it was?"

"We don't know yet," she says. "But we'll find out."

"Promise?"

Joyce turns around to look at him. "I'll promise if you'll promise me something."

Donovan looks at her warily.

"Deal?"

He doesn't respond.

"A promise works two ways, Donovan. If you want me to do something for you, you've got to do something for me."

"What?" he says.

"I want you to promise me you won't skip school anymore."

He looks at her but doesn't agree. They sit staring at each other.

"You know, I have a son. My house was nothing like yours. I don't know how your parents had four boys. One was enough for me." She chuckles, and Donovan relaxes, looking less defensive. "When he was in high school, about your age, he started skipping class. I'd get calls from the school telling me, and I'd confront him. He'd get mad." She shakes her head. "I tried everything to get him to go, but his grades started slipping. We grounded him. We'd drive him to school and wait until he entered the building. But he'd sneak out the other end and be gone." Her eyes get a faraway look. "He was hanging around with some friends that weren't a wonderful influence. Finally, one day, I got a call from the police captain. It was in the middle of the day. He wanted me to come to investigate the scene of an accident. When I got there, I recognized the car. It was my husband's. My son was in the back of a police car." She turns around and looks at Donovan. "The truck had hit a pedestrian and killed her. My son was driving, and he had been drinking. He was skipping school when it happened." Now there's an edge to her voice. "Promise me you won't skip school anymore, Donovan."

Donovan looks away. He still seems unconvinced. Joyce continues to watch him while Hank looks in the mirror.

"Donovan," Hank says, "why is he bullying you?"

A tear rolls down Donovan's cheek. "I don't know."

"Do you think it's because you're different?"

"Maybe."

Hank turns his head to look at him. "Do you think I'm different?"

Donovan frowns and doesn't know what to say.

"Do I look different?"

Donovan looks at Joyce, but she says nothing.

"How many people like me do you see around Idaho Falls?"

"None."

Hank nods. "Do you think that's hard? Do you think it's hard not to look like everyone else?"

Donovan tilts his head. "Yeah."

"You bet it is. But you know why I stay?"

"Why?"

"Because I like my job. I like my girlfriend. I like Idaho Falls. I don't enjoy being different, and I don't like being stared at by everyone. But I'm not going to let that ruin my life or what I have. Don't let that bully ruin yours."

Donovan considers that, then looks at Joyce. "I promise," he says.

Joyce smiles. "Good, now go to class."

Hank gets out of the car and opens the door for Donovan, and he climbs out. He looks up at Hank, then throws his arms around him. Hank holds him for several seconds, then lets go. When Donovan passes Joyce, he stops. "I'm sorry about your son."

Joyce nods. "Thank you. But don't be sorry for him. Be sorry for the girl he hit."

They stare at each other, then Donovan walks up the steps to the building and enters.

Joyce leans against the car, and Hank stands looking at the building. He kicks a pebble on the road. "Where is he now?"

She sighs. "Boise. He's in the state facility."

Hank nods as if he's just put something together. "How much longer?"

"Two more years." Joyce looks up at him, then at the school. "Let's go talk to that principal again. I think it's about time he protects his students."

Chapter 27

I focus my mind and return to the hospital. Ginger, my nurse, is in the room talking to James.

"Do you think you could help me?"

James sets his phone on the chair next to him and stands.

"We need to move her so she doesn't get bedsores."

I see trepidation in his movements.

"Okay, we're going to move her so that she faces me. Now, we need to be gentle, because she has several broken bones. I'm going to stand on this side of the bed. I want you to go to the other side."

James does as he's told.

"We're going to keep her head on the pillow but turn her body toward me. I'm going to pull while you push. Place one hand on her shoulder, the other on her hip. When I say push, give her some support, and I'll do the rest." Ginger grips my arm above the elbow, but James doesn't move. "What's wrong?"

James looks at me, then at her. "Does it matter?"

Ginger releases my arm and steps back. "What do you mean?"

James watches her, and when he speaks, his voice is resigned. "The doctors say she's not going to wake again."

"Is that what they said?"

He shrugs.

"Have you made your decision?"

He looks away.

"If you have, we don't have to move her. But if you haven't, there's still a chance she might wake, and my job is to care for her to the end, no matter how bad it looks. So you tell me, have you decided?"

He takes a deep breath and shakes his head.

She nods. "Okay, then help me out with her."

Ginger grabs my arm and supports my body with the other. James extends his hands and places them on me. When he does, I feel something. For the first time since waking outside my body, his touch links me to my physical form. They gently push and pull my body until Ginger is satisfied. "Thank you," she tells him, and he goes back to sit down.

Ginger rearranges the sheets and adjusts the pillows, then checks the machines and exits, closing the door behind her. James sits staring out the window, then looks at me and stands. He approaches the bed and extends his hand. His fingers whisk over my skin, and I feel an electric impulse. In a low voice, almost a whisper, he speaks to me. "What should I do? Should I turn them off?" He stares at me as if waiting for a response. "I don't know how much longer I can do this. I can't stand seeing you like this. But...I can't let go."

He moves his hand away, crosses his arms, and looks out the window. "Did you know, somehow? Did you know this would happen? Is that why you've been so distant?" He looks back down at my body. "Were you preparing me for this?"

There's a soft knock at the door, and James turns around. A thin man with curly silver hair and a slight silver beard pokes his head into the room. "James?"

I can see from James's expression that he doesn't know him. "Yes?"

The man opens the door and steps inside, closing it behind himself. He takes a few steps forward and extends his hand. "I'm Mark from Symbiotic."

Surprise registers on James's face. "Oh...hello."

Mark uses his other hand to pat James's arm. "I'm so sorry. I wanted to come out and see you and Rita as soon as I could." He looks past James at me and releases his hand. He takes a deep breath, looking down at me. "Oh, Rita," he says, shaking his head.

The two men stand side by side, looking at me.

"Any change?" Mark asks.

James shakes his head.

Mark looks away from me to James. "Can I buy you a coffee? Could we go down to the cafeteria for a few minutes?"

"Sure."

Mark leads him out, and they walk down the hall to the elevator.

"I can't imagine what you're going through," Mark says and pushes the call button. "How are the kids holding up?"

The elevator arrives, and they step inside. Mark pushes the button for the main floor.

"They're doing okay. None of us knows what to do."

Mark nods and looks down, then shakes his head, sighing. "I couldn't believe it when I got the call. I thought it was some kind of sick joke."

"It wasn't," James says with an awkward chuckle.

They reach the ground floor and step out. Mark seems as if he knows exactly where he's going and leads while James follows. They reach the cafeteria, and Mark says, "Get anything you like. We could go somewhere else if you'd rather?"

James shakes his head. "This is fine. I like to stay close. Plus, I'll need to leave soon. I've got to figure out dinner for the boys."

James grabs some Cheetos and a bottle of water. Mark gets some coffee. They go past the cashier and Mark pays, carrying the tray.

"Can we sit?" he asks, motioning toward a table in the back. The cafeteria is nearly empty other than an older couple sitting at a table in the center and a couple of nurses in scrubs.

They sit, and James opens his bag of Cheetos, taking one out and crunching down on it.

"I know this is probably the last thing on your mind right now, but I wanted to talk with you about BEAU."

James nods, chewing on his Cheetos.

"If Rita doesn't.... Well, if...," he ducks his head and whispers, "if she doesn't make it, you'll own the majority of BEAU. Have you thought about what you want to do with it?"

James looks down at his bag of Cheetos and pulls out another. "Not very much."

Mark leans back in his chair and takes a sip of coffee. "I'm sure you know we were all set to take it public. There were only a few t's to be crossed and i's to be dotted. Without Rita, those plans couldn't go forward. I won't pretend that wasn't a crushing disappointment to me and my partners. We would have made millions."

James nods. "Us too."

"Oh, for sure." Mark leans forward and puts his hand on the table. "That's what I wanted to talk to you about. I have a proposal."

James opens his water bottle and takes a few gulps.

"I want to buy you out of BEAU, and I think you'll like the amount we're willing to offer."

"How much?"

Mark taps his fingers on the table. "Three hundred million dollars."

James crunches on another Cheeto. "Rita said the public offering valued the company at a billion."

"That was *with* Rita. Plus, that's the whole value of the company. Rita...well, now you own sixty-seven percent. We own the other thirty-three."

James watches him.

"Keep in mind, without Rita at the helm, we're going to have to find another CEO and rebuild the company. It might never reach that billion again."

James nods and picks up another Cheeto in his cheesy fingers.

"Think about it, you can walk away with three hundred million. You and your boys will be set for life. That's generational wealth. Anything you want to do, you can."

"One problem, though; Rita's still alive, and I don't own the company."

Mark looks out across the cafeteria. "When this happened to Rita, I reached out to several doctors I know. They connected me with some of the foremost brain injury doctors in the country. They investigated Rita's accident and diagnosis." Mark shakes his head and looks squarely at James with his blue eyes. "Only one of them gave her any chance to live, and that one said she'd have significant brain damage. None of them gave her any chance to come back to BEAU and resume her duties as CEO." His voice grows softer. "Look, I know how hard it must be to turn off the machines. To give up on your wife. But every day this goes by, the value of BEAU drops. Not to mention what it must be doing to you and your kids."

James eyes him, and I can see Mark has reached him.

"Listen, I'll be around Idaho Falls until tomorrow night, then I need to get back to New York. If you decide to move forward, we can get the papers signed, and I can get you the money before I leave. The amount stays at three hundred million until then. After that," he shakes his head, "we may look to liquidate our portion and get out."

Chapter 28
Ethan

"What does she look like?"

Ethan Stone, field reporter for KIDK 3, looks over at his cameraman, Colby, as they sit in the news van. "I stalked her on social media."

"That's not what I asked," Colby says.

Ethan smiles. "Based on the pictures, you're going to like what you see."

Colby glares at him and pulls his cell phone from his pocket. He opens his favorite social media app. "What's her name?" he says, scrolling to the search field.

"Don't bother. She's right there."

Colby looks up to see two women exiting the office complex. One is in her mid twenties with long golden-blonde hair. The other, taller and a few years older, has long light-brown hair that gleams in the setting sunlight. From where he sits, the two could be the most beautiful women in Idaho.

"Which one?" he says, but Ethan has already exited the vehicle.

Colby opens his door and heads to the back of the van to get his camera.

Ethan strides confidently toward the taller of the two women as they separate. "Erin Callahan?" Ethan says as she looks up and sees him bearing down on her. She frowns and holds her purse tightly. "I'm Ethan Stone, reporter with KIDK 3 news."

Erin nods as Colby walks up to join them.

"Where do you want to do this?" Erin asks.

"How about right here with the BEAU office building in the back?"

Erin nods and drops her voice to just above a whisper. "Like I told you on the phone, I want it to seem like you approached me."

Ethan holds up both hands. "Oh, it will. Nobody will know you called me."

Erin looks over, checking to be sure the other woman is gone.

"Why don't you head back to the building? I'll approach you as if you're leaving work for the night."

Erin looks at him, then back to the building. "Okay. Should I go in?"

"Nah." He motions with his head for her to follow him as he approaches the entrance doors. "Just stand here. Colby will signal when you should start walking. I'll approach after you start moving away. No one will suspect it's staged. Just act as if you're leaving for the day."

Erin nods, and Ethan takes a microphone from Colby as Colby shoulders the camera. Colby presses several buttons and adjusts the camera, finally looking at Ethan.

"Ready?"

Colby nods and motions to Erin, and she walks away from the building.

"Erin Callahan?" Ethan asks as he approaches. "You're Rita Burch's assistant, aren't you?"

Erin stops and looks at him, then takes a step back. "Yes," she says warily.

"Do you have any comment about the news today regarding Rita?"

Erin frowns. "What news?"

"People say that Rita's machines are going to be turned off tomorrow."

"How did you know that?"

Ethan takes a step closer to her. "So, they *are* going to be turned off?"

Erin shakes her head. "I...that's not something I can comment on."

"Okay, maybe you can tell us how the business is doing without Rita?"

"Fine. It's hard not having her around."

"Why's that?"

Erin shrugs. "Nobody has the authority to decide without her. There are some important things that remain on hold."

"Like what?"

Erin shakes her head and waves the microphone away. "I can't comment any further."

Colby swivels to catch Erin as she walks toward the parking lot, then turns off the camera. "That's good," he calls to her. She stops and turns around, walking back to join them.

"Did it seem believable?" Erin asks Colby.

He nods. "For sure."

"When will it air?" she asks Ethan.

"Tonight, at ten."

Chapter 29

Rita

After talking to Mark, James came back upstairs to my hospital room. He sat, swiping on his phone, then left. I didn't go with him. I stayed in my room, looking at myself and thinking.

Since waking outside my body, a question has nagged at me. What would become of me? If the machines turn off, and I stop breathing, will I cease to exist? Is there a heaven? Is there a hell? Which one would I go to? I'm not a good person. There's plenty of evidence to prove that. My kids resent me, my coworkers despise me, and my sister thinks I'm an unforgiving shrew. Even my neighbors, people I had brief interactions with, called me a she-devil. I can't think of a single person who likes me. Except for James.

But does James still love me? Or does he love the idea of me? I know he felt something swiping through his phone looking at pictures. I could see it in his eyes. He loved me once, but does he still?

He shouldn't. He's better off without me. James, the only non-paid person who comes to see me every day, deserves better. I look at myself and want to scream in frustration. I hate the body before me, the person I became. I couldn't forgive my father for cheating, and I turned around and did the same thing.

My thoughts drift back to Mark. He made a compelling case for James. James would be a fool not to agree, wouldn't he? Three hundred million dollars. That's what he offered. That amount of money is life-changing. With that money, James and the boys would never have financial concerns. Anything they wanted, they could buy. It's my legacy.

I move closer to my body and watch the ventilator pump air into my lungs. Will James turn it off tomorrow? Will I die? Like before, I wonder, does everyone stuck in a coma have an out-of-body experience like this? Or is this unusual? I don't remember hearing of anyone experiencing something like this. But, then again, I remember little.

Suddenly, the room feels like it's suffocating me. I want to leave. I concentrate my thoughts on Hank and Joyce, and I'm with them. They sit in the car, parked on the side of the road. Rock music hums from the speakers. The sun is setting, but their headlights aren't on. The car sits along the curb two houses down from mine. James's white Tahoe pulls into the driveway. He opens the garage door, parks inside, then closes the door. I don't think he saw the detectives.

A minute later, a woman appears on the sidewalk. She's wearing conservative heels, a pencil skirt, and a lacy, pink top. The top is sheer, and her black bra is visible.

"Hmm," Hank says, watching her as she reaches the steps to my home.

"Is something going on between them?" Joyce asks.

Hank shrugs. "If there is, they've done a good job of hiding it."

She's carrying two large bags and walks up the steps. Something burns within me, and I leave the detectives and follow the woman. She reaches the front door, sets down one bag, and rings the bell. A voice announces a visitor at the front door. After a minute, James opens the door. He smiles, and she beams at him.

"I thought maybe you needed some help feeding the boys tonight."

James opens the door wider, waving her inside. "Kim, you're an absolute lifesaver. I was just looking through the fridge, trying to come up with something."

"I have a confession," she says, walking past him to the kitchen. "I didn't make it. But I ordered it and picked it up. That's all that matters, right?"

He laughs and follows her into the kitchen, watching her move.

Kim puts the two heaping bags onto the island and looks around. "Where are the boys?"

He shrugs. "Scattered. But don't worry, I'll make an announcement, and they'll come running."

She smiles, looking around the kitchen. "Well, let's get this place ready for them, then."

"Thank you," he says, and their eyes lock.

She moves to him and gently grabs his arm. "Come here," she says and leads him to the table. She pushes him toward the chair that faces the kitchen. "Sit. You've been through so much. Let me help you."

He looks at her and obeys, sitting down at the kitchen table. She smiles and walks back to the counter, her body swaying as she walks, her heels lightly clicking on the wood floor. She looks back and sees he's watching her. "Do you have plates?" He points to a cabinet by the stove. She glides to it and reaches up, her short blouse rising to expose a portion of soft skin near her belly. She walks back to the table and places a plate at each seat. Six total. "How did it go today?" she asks, brushing past him. She opens and closes drawers.

James looks down at the plate in front of him and runs his fingers through his hair. "It was tough. The doctors examined her again."

Kim finds the silverware and holds six knives, six forks, and six spoons in her hands and walks back to the table.

"And what did they say?"

James looks up and rubs at the back of his neck. "No improvement. They encouraged me to turn off the machines."

She freezes and looks at him. She was setting silverware around the place settings and frowns. "How soon?"

He shakes his head. "Maybe tomorrow. I just don't know if...if I can. I don't know if it's right."

She resumes placing the silverware and walks back to the food on the counter. "You need to eat. Give yourself a rest from your worries." She tears into the bags. "I hope you like Chinese. I wasn't sure, so I got a bunch of options. There's beef, chicken, shrimp, noodles, rice, you name it. What do you normally drink?"

"Rita doesn't like the boys having soda. We only have water and milk."

She smiles. "Water it is."

She fills six cups with water and ice and places them in front of the plates on the table. "Do you want to call them? Or should I?"

"Alexa," he says, "make an announcement."

A robotic voice sounds from the speaker on the counter. "What's the announcement?"

"Boys, we've got dinner. Come up and eat."

Gilbert is the first to arrive. He greets his father and looks at the food on the table.

"Have anything you want," Kim says. "Do you like Chinese?"

He scrunches his face, and James stands, putting an arm around him. "Come on, try some. And if you eat enough, I'll let you have one of the stale cookies with a secret message inside."

Gilbert looks at him and rolls his eyes. "A fortune cookie, Dad?"

One by one, the other boys come and fill their plates. Kim sits with them, opposite James. She talks to the boys, asking about their day and school. After they finish, they disappear again, separating into different corners of the house. James and Kim are left at the table.

"They're good boys," she says.

"They are."

She rises from the table and starts clearing the food.

James stands. "You don't have to do that. I'll take care of it."

She shakes her head. "No, you sit back down. I want to help."

He ignores her and starts clearing the table. She goes to the sink and starts washing the plates and the rest of the dishes and begins loading the dishwasher. Several times James sneaks glances at her. Her skirt is tight, and she has a striking figure. It's clear she takes care of herself. When they finish, they awkwardly stare at each other, only a few feet apart.

"I should go," she says.

James nods, and she walks toward the entrance. When she reaches the front door, she stops and turns around.

"There's something I wanted to tell you in private." She points to the couch in the living room. "Can we sit for a minute?"

James nods and follows her. She sits on the couch, and when he's seated, she slides closer.

"What is it?" James asks.

She looks back toward the entrance, then at him, and speaks in a low voice. "There's something I think you need to know. It's about Rita. But before I tell you, I just want you to know that I'm here for you. Whatever you need."

No! Please, don't.

"Thank you...," James says.

She clasps her hands and holds them in her lap. She looks down and hesitates, and I feel dread welling up. "I found out a few weeks ago that Rita was having an affair."

James's jaw tightens, and he looks away from her and out the window. Kim looks up from her hands and watches him.

"How do you know?" he asks, his voice hard.

"I saw her with him."

He looks back at her, clenching and unclenching his fist. "With who?"

"Bob Love."

James swallows and raises his fist to his mouth. He bites so hard on his knuckles that when he pulls his hand away, impressions of his teeth remain on his skin.

"I'm sorry," Kim says. "I wanted to tell you. I thought you should know. But then her accident happened..."

He nods and looks back out the window.

"Where did you see them?"

"They were at the Shilo Inn. I saw her first. I thought it was odd, then I saw him a few minutes later. I followed him. He went to a room, and she opened the door."

James turns back to her. "Did she see you?"

Kim shakes her head. He turns away, and she watches him. She reaches out a hand and puts it on his knee. "I'm sorry, James. I just thought you should know."

Chapter 30

After Kim tells James about my affair, he shows her to the door and she leaves. When the door shuts, James stands still, unmoving. His gaze is fixed on the back of the house, but his eyes aren't focused on anything.

After several seconds, he returns to the couch in the living room and pulls his phone from his pocket. He opens the Facebook app on his home screen and searches for Robert Love. Several options show, and he scans through them, eventually clicking on one. The profile is set to private, and after a couple of seconds, he closes the app and opens his internet browser. Again, he searches for Robert Love but adds the word *construction*.

A text comes in from Erin Callahan. James ignores it and scans the search results, then clicks on a website. The website features photos of beautiful homes around Idaho Falls. Several have similarities to ours. He navigates to the "contact" page and finds a phone number and corporate address. He mutters a stream of obscenities, then flips to another page on the site. There's a staff photo with Bob standing in the middle. James glares at the photo, his jaw working. Finally, he stands and ascends the stairs. I expect him to enter our bedroom, but he walks down the hall and opens the door to the office. He sits down at the desk and pulls open the top drawer. Inside, he finds a file and flips it open.

The pages have the same logo at the top as the one on Bob's website. James scans the papers and stops, his finger below a phone number. He dials the number into his phone and waits. After several rings, the voicemail picks up. It's an automated message repeating the phone number, then asking the caller to leave a message. James doesn't hang up but also doesn't speak. He sits, breathing into the phone. Finally, he hangs up and goes back to scanning the papers.

He flips through the pages but can't seem to find what he's looking for and goes back to his phone. He reopens the browser and types "business license lookup" into the search engine. He clicks on the first entry, Division of Occupational and Professional Licenses, arrives at the search page, and enters the required information. The page loads with license information and a physical address. He opens another window in the browser and pulls up Bob's website. He compares the two addresses, then smiles and stands from the desk. He descends the stairs, then goes down to the basement. He walks through the family room area and passes Donovan, who's playing a video game.

"Oh, hi Dad."

"Hey."

James enters through a door I've never seen opened. He flips on the light, and it's a storage room with large shelves. He walks to the back and bends down to a safe. He enters a code, and the safe opens.

Inside the safe are several guns. James pulls out a pistol and loads bullets into it. He closes the safe and exits the room.

"Whatcha doing?" Donovan asks, while keeping his eyes on the screen.

"I've got to go run an errand. I'll be back later."

"Okay."

James heads up the stairs and goes to the garage. He opens the overhead door as he walks to the Tahoe. He gets in, pulls out of the driveway, and speeds away.

It's full dark now, and James taps on the address, copies it, and pastes it into his maps app. He nearly runs the stop sign at the end of our block as he works on his phone. A voice directs him through the speakers as he drives, clenching and unclenching the steering wheel. After five minutes, he reaches his destination. He parks along the curb, checks the house numbers, takes several deep breaths, and exits the car. He walks up the driveway and ascends the steps to the front door. He knocks loudly and steps back. Nothing happens. He pushes the video doorbell and waits. Still nothing. He turns away, then stops. He goes to the door and tries the handle. The door opens, and he steps inside, closing it behind him.

The home is substantial—not as large as ours, but still substantial. James pulls the gun from his pocket, releases the safety, and walks down the hallway. The sound of a TV comes from the back of the house. Someone's watching a basketball game. James takes a deep breath, clenches his teeth, and steps around the corner.

Bob sits on the couch, his feet up on the coffee table. He looks over and sees James. James takes several quick steps toward him. Bob leans back into the couch, his hands up.

"Did you kill my wife?" James screams.

"Wha-what?"

"Rita Burch? Did you push her from the balcony? Did you kill her?" He steps to the couch and places the gun to Bob's forehead.

"James," a voice says from behind him. "Put the gun down."

It's Hank's voice. He aims a gun at James. Joyce is beside him.

"He killed my wife!" James screams.

"No, he didn't," Joyce says, stepping around Hank and coming forward.

"Yes, he did! He was having an affair with her. He killed her." James presses the gun harder against Bob's head.

"Yes, he had an affair with Rita. But we already cleared him. He has an alibi. He couldn't have done it, James. Put the gun down."

James stands motionless, staring at Bob. Bob's eyes are wide, and his lip is trembling.

"James, I promise you. Think of your kids. Their mother is dying. Don't make them lose their father, too. You can't do this. They need you."

James turns to look at her. Joyce steps to within two feet of him, hand extended. "Give me the gun."

James looks back at Bob, then his shoulders drop, and he pulls the gun away. He turns and hands the gun to Joyce as Hank comes forward and grabs him, pulling his hands behind his back and putting handcuffs on his wrists.

"I want to press charges," Bob shouts, coming forward.

Joyce steps in front of him. "Just go sit back down, Bobby."

Bob looks down at her and growls. "Don't call me that."

Hank leads James to the hallway and Joyce follows.

"Do you hear me? I want to press charges against him. He held a gun to my head!"

They've reached the front door of the home, and Hank stops.

"Mr. Love," Joyce says, her voice dripping with exhaustion, "I was here the whole time and never saw Mr. Burch threaten you in any way."

Bob looks at her, then at Hank. His face goes red with anger. "Are you kidding me?"

Hank shakes his head. "I never saw anything either."

Bob's face contorts with rage. "What!"

Hank opens the door and guides James out.

Bob comes forward and points at Joyce, his hand shaking. "He held a gun to me. You know he did."

Joyce shakes her head. "I'm sorry, but you're mistaken. And if you continue with these false claims, we're going to need to bring the permitting office into our investigation. I'm sure they'll be very interested in your business practices. Especially those involving balcony railing heights," she says and closes the door behind her.

Chapter 31

Hank pulls away from the house and looks in his rearview mirror at James. James is looking out the window. Hank looks at Joyce and mouths, "Reed's."

Joyce frowns at him.

Hank mimes holding a spoon and shoveling something into his mouth.

"Ah," Joyce says and touches her nose, smiling.

Hank grins and nods.

The three of them drive along for several minutes and pull into a parking lot off Highway 20. For the first time since getting in the car, James's eyes focus. Hank sees it.

"Do you like ice cream?"

"What?"

"Ice cream?"

James frowns. "Shouldn't I be going to jail?"

Joyce turns her head to look at him. "Do you want to go to jail?"

"No."

"Let's get some ice cream and talk about it. As you can see, Detective Powers can't get enough of it."

"Hey."

Joyce looks over and smiles, exiting her door. She opens the door for James, and he steps out.

"You grew up here, right, James?" Joyce says.

He nods as they walk to the front doors.

"You've been here before?"

"Yeah."

Hank holds the door open, and they all walk inside.

The ice cream parlor has a smattering of tables and a counter to the left. A bank of freezers with tubs of ice cream and milk on the right. A few young kids stand behind the counter.

"Welcome," the girl with long brown hair says.

The boy, skinny with a generous amount of acne, steps up to the freezer containing the open cartons of ice cream. He picks up a scoop and looks at them. All three stare up at the sign behind the kids.

"What can I get you?" the boy asks.

"What do you think, James?" Joyce asks.

"I don't want anything."

"Come on. Ice cream is my go-to when I get bad news. A lot of fat and sugar are the perfect cure for a bad day."

"A scoop of mint cookie," James says to the kid.

"Cup or cone?"

"Cone."

"What kind?" he asks, waving to the options on the counter.

"The plain one."

After handing the cone to James, he helps Joyce and Hank.

"All together?" the girl asks as they reach the register.

Both Joyce and James nod.

"I got it," James says and hands his credit card to the girl.

She runs it and wishes them a nice evening.

Hank and Joyce have already moved to the back table, far from the employees. The rest of the parlor is empty, it being near closing time. James sits down with them. He takes a lick of his ice cream.

"Thank you."

Joyce smiles. "You're welcome."

"How'd you know? Are you watching me?"

Hank nods. "Yep."

James tilts his head. "That's honest."

"I've been wondering something," Joyce says.

James looks at her and raises an eyebrow.

"How many gallons of milk do you go through a week?"

The question catches him off guard.

"Six people, four of them teenage boys." She pops a spoonful of Rocky Road into her mouth. "Three? Maybe four?"

"Six," James says.

Hank chuckles.

Joyce shakes her head. "That's even more than I thought. How about groceries? What do you spend in a week?"

James shrugs. "Between four and five hundred."

"A week?"

James nods.

Hank whistles. "I'd be broke."

"You and me both," Joyce says. She looks at James over her cup of ice cream. "How'd you know?"

"What?" James asks.

"Did Kim tell you?"

James nods.

"You didn't know before?"

He shakes his head. "How'd you know?"

Hank takes a pink phone from his pocket and slides it across the table.

James looks at it, then at them. "You had it this whole time?"

"We found it the morning after her fall."

James picks up the phone and looks at it. The battery is dead.

"What's on there?"

"Just as you'd expect, a story of her life. But about Bob? She deleted everything," Joyce says. "But we were able to restore a backup file."

James looks at her, urging her to go on.

"Just messages," Joyce says.

"How long?"

Joyce shrugs. "Hard to say. Several weeks."

James bites into his cone. He's eaten all the ice cream over the top. "Well, I guess that's my sign."

Joyce and Hank look at each other and then back at him.

He shrugs. "The doctors have been encouraging me to shut off the machines. I told myself I wouldn't unless something changed. A sign, I guess." He takes another bite of his cone and looks away. "I think this is it."

"How soon?"

He sighs. "Tomorrow." He shakes his head. "I can't do it anymore. Knowing now that she was cheating on me. It's the last straw. I'm ready to move on."

"I understand. But can you wait one more day?"

"Why?"

"Because if she dies, this investigation goes from attempted murder to murder. We'd like to narrow a few things down before that."

James looks at her, then at Hank. "Do you know who killed her?"

Joyce stares back at him. "We've got a pretty good idea. But James, there's something you need to know."

He looks at her expectantly.

"Rita broke it off with Bob before she fell. She felt guilty and wanted to make it work with you. You should know that."

He looks down and nods. "That doesn't change anything now."

"I understand. But I wanted you to know."

Chapter 32

After James finished talking with the detectives, they took him back to his car and he drove home. I wondered if he would call the boys together and tell them of his decision, but he didn't. Instead, he checked on them, saying goodnight, then climbed into bed and lay looking at the wall until his eyes finally closed. As I watched him, I wondered what it would be like to lie beside him again. He still hasn't touched my side of the bed. It remains just as I'd left it.

I focus on myself and return to the hospital. It's dark and quiet in this area of the ICU. The lights are low in the hallway, and nurses sit at their stations. I look at my body and realize this is my last night. James has decided. He's going to turn off the machines. What will become of me? Where will I go then? I don't blame him. I'd do the same thing if I were him.

As I stare at my broken body, another thought comes to me. Joyce asked him for one more day. The detectives think they knew who tried to kill me. Who? What do they know that I don't?

When they had their big meeting with the captain and the other members of their team, they listed their suspects. James, Steve (my father), Kim (my good friend and neighbor), David (my oldest),

Donovan (my second son), Erin (my assistant), Grace (my sister), and Bob (the builder and the man I was having an affair with). Who among them could it be?

I never thought it was James. He was taking the kids to school when it happened. I suppose he could have come back, pushed me off, then called 9-1-1. Except Donovan said he saw me already lying on the patio before James came back. Plus, James is the only person who has come to see me every day. If there's anyone who truly loves me, it's him. When I learned I was a cheater, it cast more suspicion on him. But it's clear now that he didn't know about my infidelity. His reaction when Kim told him was genuine. I don't believe it's him. Plus, he's been in here with me so many times—*alone*. If he wanted to hurt me, he could have.

Steve, my father, had both motive and opportunity. He was home alone when the accident happened. James had been giving him money without my knowledge. If I was out of the way, he could pester James unceasingly. Then again, if he had only waited a week or two, James would have had more money than anyone in the state. He could have given Steve millions without batting an eye. The detectives also didn't seem to think it was him.

What about Kim? She had opportunity. She was home with her daughter when it happened. James came and picked her son up for school. She could have snuck over to my house and returned without her daughter knowing. Then she took her to school, all before James came back. But that doesn't seem likely. Plus, what was her motive? It's not like she'd get money from me. We were friends. She was my only friend. But why did she tell James about my affair? Was it simply a secret she had to get out? It wouldn't make sense for it to be her. Would it?

I never believed it could be one of my sons. Yes, David was angry with me, but killing his own mother? Plus, he was in school when it happened. He had a rock-solid alibi. If it was one of them, it was Donovan. He didn't have an alibi. He wasn't in school. He admitted to being home around the time of the accident. Still...killing his own mother? I can't believe he'd do that.

What about Erin? She was supposed to be on a call with me, but because I was the organizer, and I never signed on, there's no way to prove she was. She had opportunity, but what motive? She was about to get what she wanted. She was going back home to New York. When the company went public, Symbiotic planned to liquidate their shares and reassign Erin. She'd be free of me. There'd be no reason to kill me. Unless...what if she was lying? What if she really didn't want to leave? Donovan said he thought the person hiding was a woman. Maybe it was her... And what about that text? She texted James last night. What did it say?

The last two suspects were Grace and Bob. I can't see a motive for either. Maybe money for Grace, but she had an ironclad alibi. She was at a doctor's appointment for Rachel. It couldn't have been her. Bob was at a networking meeting with other local businesspeople. He could have snuck out, but unlikely. Plus, his only conceivable motive would have been to take his anger out on me. I don't think he was angry. I believe what he said. I was just another tick on his bedframe.

I look out the window, stare at the moon, and realize this might be my last time. Tomorrow night, I'll likely be dead. Whoever it was will have won. I look back at my body and wish I could scream. I've got to do something. I've got to find and expose them. I don't need to live, but I can't stand the thought of being dead while my killer goes free.

Chapter 33

I spent the rest of the night wishing it could last but eager for it to end. When the light finally peaked out over the mountaintop, I knew where I wanted to go. Mark.

He wasn't on the suspect list. But the more I thought about it, the more I became convinced he should've been. True, he was in New York when I fell. He couldn't have pushed me. But he could have been working with someone. Or even hired them. He potentially had the most to gain. Even more than James. If he had me killed, then he could do just what he did to James. Offer him a dollar amount that could be millions or billions in discount. I had to find out.

I concentrate my mind and find him. He's at the Hilton Garden Inn, seated in the breakfast area. He's reading the *Wall Street Journal* on his phone and sipping a cup of coffee.

A tall, lean woman with long light-brown hair and soft curls enters the hotel through the automatic glass doors. She removes her sunglasses and looks around, trying to get her bearings. She sees him to her right and walks through the smattering of people sitting at tables. Several heads turn, gawking in her direction, but Mark doesn't even look until she's reached his table.

"Oh, Erin, sit down." He motions toward the seat opposite him, and she puts her bag on the unoccupied chair and sits, smiling at him.

"It's good to see you in person. Not through a computer screen."

He chuckles. "One thing I can't quite get used to in this world we're in now. I seem to see myself on a computer screen more than I look in the mirror."

A worn man in an all-black outfit stands at their table. He's wearing a name tag and greets Erin.

"Miss, can I get you something to drink? Coffee? Tea? Orange Juice?" He hands her a menu.

Erin looks up at him and smiles. "Coffee, please."

He smiles and leaves, and Erin turns back to Mark. "When did you get in?"

"Yesterday. I had to fly into Salt Lake City and drive up. That was about three hours. Pretty country, but inconvenient."

Erin nods, and the server brings her a coffee. She opens a sugar packet and sprinkles it into the cup. "How long are you staying?"

Mark tips his shoulder. "That depends. How are things at BEAU?"

Erin picks up a small cup of cream and dumps it in her coffee, then stirs it. "Good. Obviously, without Rita, we had to make some adjustments, but I've been able to talk with our suppliers in China and Indonesia. I reassured them, and things have carried on as usual. Retailers are concerned, but we've been working to calm their fears.

Sales have been better than ever. I think all the news coverage has made the brand even more coveted. I'm not sure how long that will last, but for now, things are good."

Mark nods and looks up as the server returns.

"Have you decided on breakfast?"

Mark looks down at his menu. "I feel like I should have potatoes. First time in Idaho, and you guys are famous for them, but I don't see any on the menu."

The server takes his menu and turns it over. "There's a backside as well. Several of the kitchen specials have breakfast potatoes."

"Oh," Mark says, adjusting the distance of the menu and squinting. "I'll have the Snake River Breakfast Skillet. Isn't that the river over there?" Mark waves a hand to his right.

"It is," the man says and writes the order on a small notepad. "You, miss?"

Erin smiles at him. "Greek-yogurt bowl, please."

"The berries are strawberries and blueberries. Is that okay?"

"Great!"

He makes a note, smiles at her again, and leaves.

Mark sits back in his chair and raises his coffee cup. "Funny you should mention the uncertainty over there right now. When I got to town, I went straight to the hospital and saw James. Well, Rita too." He pauses and looks down. "James confided the doctors are encouraging him to shut off the machines."

Erin says nothing, only watching him, her face grave.

"So, I made him an offer."

A woman a few tables over cackles with laughter and Mark pauses. Seeing it has nothing to do with them, he leans forward. "I offered to purchase the company outright. Buy out Rita's portion and help him move on. The only problem is that until he turns off the machines, he doesn't own the company. He can't sell until Rita is no longer breathing."

The server returns, and Mark holds out his coffee cup. He tops it off and offers the same to Erin, but she shakes her hand and he leaves.

Mark puts his cup on the table and crosses his arms. "I've given him until tonight to respond to my offer."

"Can I ask what the offer was?"

"Three hundred million. As you know, the valuation had it over a billion when taking it public, but without Rita, that value will be much less. Which brings me to you."

Erin's eyes go wide, and she takes a sip of her coffee.

"If he accepts our offer, I'd like to name you as CEO of BEAU." He stops and watches her, a sly smile creeps along his lips.

"Me?" Erin says breathlessly. She sits back and looks down, eyes on her coffee.

"To say it will be challenging would be a severe understatement. For all of Rita's faults, she was a hell of a businesswoman. But I can't think of anyone more qualified."

Erin takes several deep breaths, her cheeks full of color.

"Now, understand, we have no intention of running a clothing brand forever. Our business is purchasing, growing, and liquidating businesses for a handsome profit. Your mandate will be to get us back to that billion-dollar-or-more valuation. Once we reach that, we take the company public and sell our shares. You'd no longer be a Symbiotic employee, and you'd likely remain as CEO of BEAU."

Erin looks away, her mind working. "Would I have to stay here?"

Mark shakes his head. "That would be up to you, but I don't see any reason you would. It would be wise to stay at least a few weeks, but then, I don't see why you couldn't come back to the city."

Erin smiles, and the server returns. He places the yogurt in front of her, then gives Mark the skillet.

"Would you like any hot sauce?"

"Do you have Cholula?" Mark asks.

"Sure. Anything else?"

Mark looks at Erin, and she smiles and shakes her head.

The server nods and walks away.

"Now, if this happens, you'll no longer be a Symbiotic employee. You'll become an employee of BEAU and earn the same salary Rita was earning, which was one-point-five million before bonuses."

Erin smiles and chuckles softly.

Mark grins. "Congratulations."

"Thank you," she says, then frowns. "Do you think James will sell?"

Mark shrugs. "What other choice does he have? He can't run the company. His only other option is to find someone to run it, and if that happens, we'll pull our support and sell our interest."

Erin takes a small spoonful of yogurt. "So, we wait?"

Mark nods. "Unless you have some way to get him to do it before tonight."

Chapter 34

The breakfast didn't last much longer. Mark received a call and covered the phone while telling Erin he needed to take it. She took the hint and left. Mark went upstairs to his hotel room, fired up his laptop, and got to work.

I wondered what James and the boys were doing and concentrated my mind and found them in the house. James is sitting at the kitchen table, and David comes up the stairs wearing only his underwear, rubbing the sleep from his eyes.

"Dad." He looks around the kitchen. "What's going on? Why didn't you wake us up?"

James pats the table next to him. David comes over and sits down.

"Do you want some cereal?"

David leans back in the chair and yawns. "Sure."

"What kind?" James stands from the table and walks over to the pantry.

"Cocoa Pebbles."

James shakes his head, grabs the box, goes to the fridge and gets the milk, then puts the box and jug in front of David. He walks to the cabinets, gets a couple of bowls and spoons, and sits back down beside him. David fills both bowls and James pours the milk.

"Dad," David says. "Can I ask you something?"

"Sure," he says, taking a spoonful of Cocoa Pebbles.

"Is this about Rita?"

"Is what about Rita?"

"The reason you didn't get us up for school today."

They stare at each other, and finally James looks away and takes another spoonful of cereal.

"Have I ever told you when I realized I loved your mom?"

David shakes his head.

"We met in college. She was a couple of years younger. I had a friend who was dating a girl on the soccer team. I went to a game and saw your mom. She was playing in the game."

"Rita played college soccer?"

"She was an elite athlete. A better athlete than me. Have you ever seen a girl you just felt drawn to? Not just beautiful, but a deep attraction? Like you couldn't get her off your mind?"

David nods.

James's eyebrows raise. "Really? Well, we'll have to talk about her later. This is my story..."

David smiles.

"After the game, my friend introduced me to his girlfriend, and your mom came over to talk to her. I don't know what came over me, but I *had* to talk to her."

"What did you say?"

"Good game."

They both laugh.

"I know, really eloquent. Anyway, she smiled, thanked me, and probably rolled her eyes after walking away. I went back to talking with my friend and his girlfriend. They were discussing a party that night, and I had to go, hoping your mom would be there. I needed another chance. When I saw her at the party, I repeated what I'd said when we met. *Good game.* She laughed, and we started talking. After a few minutes, I asked her out, and she said yes." James holds up a finger. "But that's not when I fell in love with her."

"So when was it?"

"We dated for a few months, and although I was crazy about her, I felt like I was missing the college experience. I wasn't dating other girls. My buddies would tease me about missing out, and I thought maybe I was. So, I broke up with her."

"You did?"

James nods. "The very next day, she came over to the place I was working as a server. She sat in my section. I won't lie. I held my breath as I went over to take her order."

David's watching him intently. "What happened?"

James smiles. "When I went up to her, tears were streaming down her face. I was alarmed and sat down across the table from her and asked what was wrong."

"What did she say?"

"She told me she knew we were supposed to be together, that she loved me. Although I was touched, I wasn't convinced. I told her I still needed time. She left, and I went on dates with other girls over the next couple of weeks." James shakes his head and chuckles. "The whole time I wanted to be with your mom. After the second or third date, I knew, like she did, we were meant to be together. Two weeks later, we were engaged."

David smiles and picks up his bowl and drinks the milk.

James reaches out and puts a hand on David's shoulder. "I know you're angry with her, and you have every right to be. I'm angry too. She hasn't been the same person for the last few years. But I know she loves you, son. Remember the mom she was before BEAU."

James hugs him, and after a few seconds, they part.

"Will you do me a favor?"

David nods.

"Will you wake up your brothers? There's something I need to tell all of you."

David stands from the table, and James gets more bowls and spoons and places them at the other seats. One by one, the other boys enter the kitchen, rubbing sleep from their eyes. James hugs each one and pours them cereal. When they're all seated, he stands at the end of the table. "Guys, I didn't have you go to school today because I've made a decision. I want you all to go to the hospital with me. So, eat your cereal, then go shower. I'd like to be there around ten."

"Is something happening?" Donovan asks.

"I just think we need to spend the day together as a family." The boys look at each other, then back at him. "I've already called your schools and excused your absences."

"I'm gonna go shower," David says.

The rest of the boys pour themselves cereal.

A few minutes later, the doorbell rings. James looks at his phone, sees the person standing on the porch, and walks to the door. When he opens it, a tall, beautiful blonde is at the entrance.

"Erin?"

"Hi, James."

They stare at each other.

"Sorry to come unannounced. I wanted to check in on you. Do you have a minute?"

James nods and shows her into the living room. She sits on the couch.

"I'll be right back." James leaves her, tells the boys to get ready, then returns. "Sorry about that." He sits down in the chair opposite her. "What's up?"

"I wanted to come by and see how you're doing. You never responded to my text last night."

James's mouth drops open. "Oh, that's right. You texted me. I saw but never read the text. Sorry, I had a lot going on."

She smiles. "No problem. So you didn't see the news?"

"The news?"

"Yeah, a TV reporter stopped me outside the office. They reported you were turning off the machines today."

James frowns. "What? How?"

"I don't know. They surprised me, and I didn't know what to say. I could have handled it better. I'm sorry."

James sits back in his chair and blows out a breath of air.

"Is it true?"

He shrugs. "How are things at the company?"

Erin shakes her head. "Honestly, not very good. Things are kind of a mess since Rita's accident."

James frowns. "Really?"

"Yeah, we've lost some big clients. I'm kind of scared."

James sighs. "Oh...I'm sorry."

"Yeah," she says, looking down. "I'm afraid to tell Mark."

"He's in town."

"What?"

"Yeah, he came into town yesterday. He stopped over to the hospital to see Rita. You didn't know?"

She shakes her head. "He's probably come to fire me."

"It's that bad over there?"

She sighs. "I don't know. So, do you think you're going to turn off the machines?"

James looks at her for a long while, then nods. "The doctors say she's brain dead. There's no hope. I can't put my boys through this anymore."

"So, what happens? What happens with the company?" As if realizing something, she puts out a hand. "I'm sorry, James. You already have so much on your mind. I don't mean to add to it. I'm just scared."

He shakes his head. "No, you don't need to apologize. It's okay. I understand. This is hard for all of us."

She nods, and they sit lost in thought.

"I guess you own BEAU then, huh?"

He shrugs.

"I mean, if..."

He looks out the window.

"Is that why Mark came?"

He looks back at her and nods. "He offered to buy me out. But I have to decide today."

"Really?"

He nods.

"What are you going to do?"

He shakes his head. "I'm not sure. But I've got to do it today. Whatever it is."

Reed comes into the room, and James looks at him.

"Dad?"

"Yeah?"

"There's something wrong with the toilet in our bathroom. Can you come and look at it?"

"Sure."

Reed looks at Erin, then walks back to the stairs.

"Sorry, Erin, duty calls."

Erin stands, and James walks her to the door. When she reaches it, she opens it and turns back to him. "If it were me, I'd take whatever Mark is offering. I just don't think the company will survive without Rita. Take what you can now."

Chapter 35

She's the one. The vulture has revealed herself. I never saw it. I never conceived of it. Now it's clear. She planned it all. She knew that with me gone, James would be forced to sell, and Mark would offer her the CEO ship. She's going to get exactly what she's wanted, and nobody is going to know or stop it. Where are Hank and Joyce? Why aren't they seeing this? I concentrate my mind and find them at the hospital. They're sitting around in a waiting room.

Joyce holds a *People* magazine in her hands. A pretty brunette is on the cover with the title "Kate Has Cancer" written in pink. The subtitle of "What Happens Next?" is in black. Hank's on his phone, playing a game.

A woman in purple scrubs comes out of the closed door and calls, "Joyce Powers." Joyce returns the magazine to the coffee table, and she and Hank follow the woman to the back. "Dr. Long asked me to find an open consultation room," she says, looking back at them over her shoulder as they walk along a narrow hallway. She stops outside an open door. "Have a seat anywhere you like. The doctor will be with you shortly."

Joyce thanks her, and she enters the room before Hank.

The room is small, with only one chair beside the examination table. The detectives look at each other, and Hank motions toward the chair. Joyce smiles and sits down. Hank walks over and sits on the examination table. The paper crinkles under his weight. His feet nearly reach the floor as he sits on the high padded table. He looks over at the opposite wall and reads the poster. It's an advertisement for prenatal vitamins.

"First time in an OBGYN examination room?" Joyce asks.

"Yep."

"Don't worry, I don't think he'll use the stirrups on you." Hank looks at the table, then reaches out a hand and pulls one of the metal pieces jutting out. He examines it, then pushes it back in. "Do you want me to tell you what those are used for?"

Hank frowns at her. "I think I can figure it out."

She smiles. "Do you want kids?"

"I think so."

"Does Saundra?"

He shrugs. "Yeah, but not as much as I do. I think she worries about it affecting her career. I try to tell her we'll figure it out together, but...we'll see."

"Sam's first time in an office like this was when I was pregnant with Jeff. He was more scared than I was."

Hank laughs, and the doctor comes in. He's an Asian man with black hair that's just going gray. He looks at Joyce. "Detective Gardener?"

She shakes her head and doesn't stand. "No, I'm Detective Powers. This is Hank Gardener."

Hank shakes the doctor's hand. The doctor looks like a child next to Hank. Dr. Long looks for a chair, but finding none, steps out into the hallway and rolls one in. He sits and looks at Hank. "Do you want a chair also?"

Hank shakes his head. "No, I'm fine here. Unless you're going to want to examine me."

Dr. Long gives him a forced smile, then turns back to Joyce. "The front desk told me you're investigating Rita Burch's accident and had some questions for me. I'm not sure what help I can be. I didn't know her well. I only saw her a few times."

"Where was that?" Joyce asks.

"Driving through the neighborhood. Once at the grocery store."

"Was she ever in your home?"

"No."

"I understand your ex-wife...," Joyce stops herself. "Your soon-to-be ex-wife and Rita were friends?"

He frowns. "Who told you that?"

"Kim."

"Hmm. I never saw them together. Kim didn't like her."

"No?"

"No. She thought she was...conceited. Looking back, I think it was jealousy."

"Why jealousy?"

"Rita's pretty. Kim always compared herself to other women. She was obsessed with it. And she always dreamed of running a business like Rita's. I think she envied her success."

Joyce nods, and Hank makes a note in his notepad.

"Can I ask why you and Kim split up?"

"I wasn't fond of my wife sleeping with other men. I don't know how many there were, but the last one was the final straw."

Joyce waits, but when it's clear he'll say nothing more, she asks, "Who was the last one?"

"The contractor who built our house."

"Robert Love?"

His eyes narrow. "I didn't like him when we hired him. Kim did. A lot..."

Hank and Joyce look at each other.

"You said you thought she was jealous of Rita. Any reason you thought that?"

He scowls. "Kim tried to start an online business as well. Hers was jewelry. She came up with some designs. I invested a bunch of money in it. She barely sold anything. There are still boxes of it in the garage. It's one item we're disputing in the divorce. I want credit for the money I invested in her failed business."

"How long ago was this?"

He pulls on his lip. "Three or four years." He holds up a hand. "This is all being disputed in our divorce. I can't have you telling people."

"Don't worry about that," Hank says. "We'll keep anything you tell us confidential."

He nods and looks down at his watch.

"Just a couple more questions, and we'll let you get back to work. Do you know if Kim is still seeing Bob?"

He shakes his head. "I don't know, and I don't care. I just want the divorce over and to move on. If she wasn't so greedy, it could have been over months ago."

"She's not happy with the financial arrangement?"

"I offered her four thousand a month in alimony, the house, and her car. She wants double that and is threatening not to allow me to see the kids."

"Can she do that?"

He shrugs. "She's trying." He shakes his head. "She's a vindictive woman. The sooner I can be rid of her, the better."

A nurse knocks on the door, and he tells her to come in.

"Doctor, your patient is waiting."

He stands from his chair. "I'm sorry, detectives. I have to go."

Joyce holds up a finger as he moves toward the door. "One more question. Does Kim iron?"

"Iron?"

"Yes, clothes."

"Yeah, I guess so."

"Did you ever see her use starch?"

"I don't know. I never paid attention."

Joyce stands. "Thank you, Doctor. We'll see our way out."

Chapter 36

Once the detectives are back in the car, Joyce pulls out her cell phone and calls Sarah, their assistant in the case.

"Sarah, I need you to do something for me. Gather as much information about Kim Long as you can. I want everything: birth records, financial information, blood type. Everything. As quick as you can."

Joyce is looking down as she holds the phone to her ear, and Hank, sitting behind the wheel, bumps her with his elbow.

"Is that it? Do you need anything else? What about—¬"

She looks over at him, and Hank points out the windshield. James is walking past with all the boys.

"Yes, sorry, Sarah. Email me when you have it." She hangs up and looks at Hank. "I thought he was going to wait until tonight?"

"Maybe he's just bringing them back to spend the day with her before he shuts off the machines."

"Let's go find out."

The detectives get out of the car and enter the hospital. James and the boys have already cleared the lobby, and they call the elevator. When they reach the second floor, they go down the hall to the waiting room and find the family inside. James is standing next to Donovan; the rest of the boys are on the couch. The detectives enter the room, and the boys, including James, look over at them. Joyce motions to James and he nods. The detectives exit the room, and James says something to Donovan, holds up a finger, and follows them out.

"Change of plans?" Joyce asks as he reaches them.

"Huh?"

"I'm just asking if anything has changed since last night."

James sighs and looks away.

"Talk to us, James," Hank says.

"Guys, I just can't do it anymore."

"What happened?" Joyce asks.

"We're tired. The uncertainty is getting to us. I just can't put the boys through it anymore. I have to pull the plug."

Joyce shakes her head, but Hank nods.

"I get it. But did something else happen since last night? What changed?" Hank asks.

James looks up at him. "Erin, Rita's assistant, came by the house. She said the company is struggling. I'm going to accept Mark's offer and sell. I can't do it until the machines are off."

Hank and Joyce look at each other.

"James," Hank says. "Just give us until three. That's all we need. Give us five hours."

James shakes his head.

"Come on, man. Just a few more hours."

James hesitates. "Grace said she can't be here until two. I'll give you until then."

"We'll take it," Joyce says.

Hank pats James on the shoulder, and the detectives walk away.

Chapter 37

I stuck around the hospital worrying James might go back on his word with the detectives. But after fifteen minutes, I grew convinced he'd give them the few hours they sought. I became more curious about where the detectives were headed next and concentrated my mind on them. They were approaching the Hilton Garden Inn along the banks of the Snake River.

After parking, they enter the hotel and walk to the front desk. A woman with large glasses greets them.

"Checking in?"

Hank shakes his head. "We're here to talk to one of your guests." He takes out his badge and shows it to her.

"Is something wrong?"

"No. We need information in an investigation, and we think one of your guests might be able to help."

"Okay."

"We need to know what room Mark Allen is staying in."

The woman nods and types on her computer. "He's in three-eleven. Would you like me to call him?"

Hank shakes his head. "Unnecessary. If we have trouble reaching him, we'll be back."

Hank and Joyce walk away and call for the elevator. After several seconds, it arrives. A family with two small children and a large stroller exits the elevator. Once they're clear, the detectives enter, and Hank presses number three.

"How do you want to handle this?" Hank asks.

"Why don't you start? I'll jump in once I get a sense of him."

The elevator reaches the third floor, and they follow the signs to room 311. A maid has the room door next to 311 open, standing at the cart. Hank nods to her, but she doesn't respond, only watches them.

Hank steps to the door and knocks. The Come Back Later sign on the doorknob shakes with the pounding. The detectives wait for a response, but none comes. The maid continues to watch them, standing at her cart.

"Is someone inside?" Hank asks, pointing to the door.

"*Qué?*" the woman asks.

"Inside? Is there someone inside?"

The woman shakes her head. "No English."

"*Hay alguien dentro?*" Joyce says.

"Oh, *sí*," she says, looking relieved. "*Un hombre de negocios.*"

"*Gracias,*" Joyce says.

"*De nada.*"

Hank looks at Joyce. "What did she say?"

"Someone is inside."

"That's all?"

"That's all I understood."

Hank smiles and turns back to the door. This time he knocks harder, rattling the walls. The sign on the doorknob falls to the floor. Joyce bends over and picks it up as the door opens. Mark stands at the entry wearing white earbuds. He looks up at Hank, then at Joyce, then past them at the maid.

"Yes?"

"Mark Allen?" Hank says.

"Yes?"

"I'm Detective Hank Gardener of the Idaho Falls Police Department. This is my partner, Joyce Powers. We're investigating the accident of Rita Burch. Do you have a few minutes?"

"What for?"

"To talk about Rita and your relationship with her. We can come in, if you like. Or we can go to the lobby, if you're more comfortable with that."

Hank and Joyce hold up their badges. He examines them, then waves his hand. "You can come in, I guess."

He has a suite with two separate rooms, separated by a double door. The door is open, and the bed is unmade, his suitcase on the ground, and there are clothes on the bed. They walk to the couch and sit. Mark has his laptop on the white desk along the wall. He sits down on the red chair beside them and takes out his headphones, putting them back in their case.

"Thank you for talking with us," Hank says. "We know you're busy."

"No problem," Mark says. "So, what's this about? Did something else happen?"

Hank ignores the question. "When did you get into town?"

"Yesterday afternoon."

"From New York?"

"Yes."

"What brought you?"

"I wanted to see Rita."

"Were you able to see her?"

"Briefly."

"How long are you staying?"

"Not much longer. Look, detectives, is something going on?"

"What do you know about Rita's accident?" Joyce asks.

"What do you mean?"

Joyce shrugs. "What have you heard about it?"

Mark takes a deep breath. "Well, Erin, Rita's assistant, called me and told me Rita had fallen, but she knew little more. The news has said it might not have been an accident. Maybe someone pushed her. I came out as fast as I could. When I saw her, it matched what James told me on the phone. She didn't look good."

"You talked to James?"

"Yes. I called him after I talked to Erin."

Joyce watches him. "How did he seem?"

Mark looks up at the ceiling. "Distraught."

"What makes you say that?" Joyce asks.

"I don't know. The way he talked. He seemed rattled."

Joyce nods. "Do you know anyone who would want to hurt Rita?"

"No."

"What about you?"

"What about me?"

"Would you want to hurt her?"

Mark's voice rises. "Are you kidding?"

"No."

He sits forward in his chair. "Why would I want to hurt Rita?"

"That's what I asked you."

He sits back and sighs. "Detectives, we bought into BEAU, the clothing company she started. Why? Because of Rita. We bought thirty-three percent of the company for thirty million dollars. We were expecting to take the company public and sell our shares for over three hundred million dollars. Now that Rita's not running the company, that opportunity is gone. From a financial standpoint, nobody lost more than me by Rita's accident."

"That's true," Hank says, looking at Joyce. "He makes a good point."

Joyce keeps her eyes on Mark. "So, what happens now with the company?"

"What do you mean?"

"Say Rita dies. What happens?"

"Based on what I know about her will, James owns her shares."

"And what does that do to your investment?"

"Cuts it in half at a minimum."

"So instead of your shares being worth three hundred million, they drop to one hundred and fifty million?"

"Or less."

Joyce shakes her head. "I don't buy it."

Mark guffaws. "What's there to buy?"

"I investigated you. You invest millions of dollars every year into new businesses. Many make huge returns. I don't believe you'd leave yourself that exposed."

"Maybe you give me too much credit."

"I don't think so."

Mark sighs and shakes his head. "When we invested in BEAU, we took out a life-insurance policy on Rita. It covers our investment. But the appreciation since acquiring our shares was going to be realized once we took it public. When she fell, so did the stock. The best thing for us would be for Rita to recover as quickly as possible."

"But what if she doesn't?"

"Then it's Plan B."

"Which is?"

"Either buy James out or find a buyer and sell now."

"How much would you buy him out for?"

He shakes his head. "As little as he'll take. I mean, I don't want to take advantage of him, but we lost so much with this accident. I'm just trying to make it hurt less."

"But if she dies, then you get the life insurance money. And then, if James sells to you, you could stand to make a lot of money."

"That's a lot of ifs."

"Seems like James hurts the most. He loses his wife and a lot of money."

Mark shrugs. "He'll be okay. He'll have more money than he can spend."

Joyce crosses her legs. "Let's say she dies and James sells to you for three hundred million. What will you do with the company?"

"Easy, hire new leadership, get the business back to the valuation or close, and go public. My job is to make our company and our investors money. I can't do that until the company sells. Appreciation in principle is great, but until it sells, it's nothing more than figures on a balance sheet. That's why the accident hurts so much. We were about to see a huge profit realized." His phone rings, and he looks at it.

"Last question."

His attention transfers back to her.

"Who do you think tried to kill her?"

He shakes his head. "At first, I thought maybe James. But after meeting him, I don't believe that. It had to be personal. Maybe someone in the family."

Hank and Joyce stand, and Mark answers his call.

"I'll call you right back."

He hangs up and shows them to the door.

Joyce turns back to him when they reach the hallway. She hands him her card. "Mark, we'd appreciate it if you'd stay until tomorrow."

He shakes his head. "I've got to get back."

"Give us until tomorrow at noon."

He looks at her and shrugs. "Fine. Noon."

"Thank you."

Chapter 38

After leaving Mark, the detectives say little inside the car. They don't even discuss where they're going. Hank drives, and Joyce looks out the window, lost in thought. After five minutes, Hank pulls the car into a professional plaza and finds a parking spot. After shutting off the car, Joyce looks at Hank.

"I'll start this time."

Hank nods, and they exit the vehicle. They enter the building, look around to get their bearings, and then walk toward an office. It's a dental practice, based on the etching in the glass. Joyce pushes open the door and Hank follows. Several women sit behind a large counter. The waiting room is full of patients sitting on an eclectic mix of seats. There are couches, wingback chairs, and a few coffee tables. Even a rocking chair that looks like it might have been from grandma's parlor back in 1912.

"Can I help you?" A pretty blond woman with short hair in her late fifties asks.

"Yes," Joyce says. "We're here to see Kim Long."

The woman turns to the dental hygienist near her. "Have you seen Kim today?"

"She's in her office."

The woman turns back to them. "Is she expecting you?" She rises from the desk.

"Please tell her Joyce Powers and Hank Gardener have a few follow-up questions for her."

The woman smiles and turns away.

"You can sit down. We'll call you when she's available," says the hygienist.

"That's okay. We'll wait right here."

The hygienist glares at her, then stands and walks away.

The woman returns. "She's coming."

Joyce thanks her, and they step back from the counter. Moments later, Kim comes through the door wearing a conservative blouse and jeans. I almost don't recognize her. *Where's the cleavage?*

"Let's go out here," she says, walking past them and pushing open the exterior door.

Joyce and Hank look at each other, then follow.

When they're all on the sidewalk in front of the building, Kim says, "I thought it might be easier to talk out here. My office is small. How can I help you? Has something happened?"

Joyce points to the park across the street. "Can we walk for a minute?"

"Sure."

After crossing the street, they walk on the grass in the park. The park is deserted, other than a runner and a couple walking a dog.

"Kim, we've learned you weren't entirely truthful with us when last we spoke."

Kim stops. "I beg your pardon?"

Joyce eyes her. "No more lies."

"What was I lying about?"

"We spoke with your husband. He doesn't remember you being friends with Rita. Quite the opposite, really. He says you hated her."

Her voice registers disgust. "He doesn't know anything."

"Why did you tell James about Rita's affair?"

"What?"

"The other night. Why did you go to the Burch home and tell James about Rita's affair with Bob Love?"

She hesitates. "I didn't."

"Really? So, it was a coincidence that James would drive over to Bob's house minutes after you left and confront him? That had nothing to do with you?"

Kim looks away.

Joyce steps closer to her. "Here's the deal, Kim. We know you were having an affair with Bob. We know your husband found out and left you. That was fine until Bob dumped you. Now you went from having two men to none. What happened then? Did you learn about Rita and Bob? Find out Bob left you for her?"

Kim looks at her with fire in her eyes. "How dare you."

Joyce's face contorts in anger. "Rita stole him from you. He liked her more. How did that feel? She had everything you wanted, and you couldn't handle it, so you killed her."

Kim's eyes go wide, and she shakes her head. "No, I didn't. I would never."

"Come on, Kim."

She holds up a hand. "No, I didn't. Yes, I had an affair with Bob, but he was nothing to me. There was no future there. I told James because I thought he should know. I saw them together in a hotel. You've met him. James is a good man. He deserved to know."

Joyce sneers. "Suddenly you have morals about affairs. I don't buy it."

"Buy what you want." She looks down at her phone. She's getting a call. "Detectives, I have to get back to work."

She moves away from them, and Joyce calls out to her.

"We're on to you, Kim. If Rita dies, this goes from attempted murder to murder. Better to confess now."

Kim shakes her head, crosses the street, and reenters the building.

Joyce looks at Hank. "She didn't crack."

He looks at the building. "She called our bluff."

"Are we wrong about her? We've got nothing concrete on her. If she did it, she's going to get away with it." Joyce stomps her foot and kicks a dandelion while growling. She clenches and unclenches her hands, takes several deep breaths, and looks up at the leaves on the trees. "Why? Why didn't she crack?"

He shrugs. "She's as cold as ice."

She looks at him and chuckles when she sees his smile. "I'll buy you a Coke if you can tell me the band."

"Easy. Foreigner."

She smacks him on the shoulder, and they walk back to the car. "I'm impressed, Detective."

He grins.

"How'd you know that?"

He opens his door. "For the last year, rock music is all you've let me listen to. I've been thinking about growing out my hair, bleaching it, and getting some tight pants. Maybe get a leather jacket."

She laughs as he starts the engine. "Saundra would love it."

"You think?"

"Oh, yeah. That's how Sam looked when I met him. I couldn't keep my eyes off his tight butt."

Hank laughs.

"Let's hit the Maverick, and I'll pay up on that Coke. Then we better get to the hospital. This is about to become a full-fledged murder investigation."

Chapter 39

How could I have forgotten? No, I didn't forget. I pushed it from my consciousness. An effort to block out reality. Pretend it wasn't happening. I allowed myself to focus on the detectives and my case rather than my broken body and fractured family. James is turning off the machines, and I don't know what will become of me.

I force myself to leave the detectives and focus on my body. When my consciousness arrives in the hospital room, I see I'm not alone. Dr. Mitchell and Ginger are there, along with another doctor I don't recognize. Dr. Mitchell holds one of my eyelids open, shining a light at my eye. She releases it, then moves to my toes, and finally my fingers. I don't know what she's hoping for, but whatever it is, I can tell from the downward lines in her face she hasn't found it.

She looks over at Ginger and the other doctor and shakes her head. Ginger frowns and looks like she might cry but holds it together.

"I'll go talk to James," Dr. Mitchell says. "If you'll prep the room."

Ginger nods, and the doctors walk down the hallway toward the waiting room. Once inside, Dr. Mitchell and James make eye contact. James stands from the couch and follows the doctors into the hallway. James looks at them hopefully.

"James, I'm sorry to say there's no change."

His face falls, and he looks down.

"Would you still like to proceed?"

"Is there any hope?"

She pauses while looking into his eyes. "I'm afraid not."

He nods, keeping his gaze on his shoes. "Let me tell the boys."

"Do you want us to arrange for another room?"

"No, the waiting room is fine. It's only our family in there now."

Dr. Mitchell nods, her face grave. "We'll be prepping her room. Come down when you're ready."

James looks at her. "What will happen?"

"To her?"

"Yes, to her body."

"After? Or during?"

"During."

"We'll remove the ventilator, and because she's brain dead, she'll die within minutes. We'll be there the whole time to monitor her."

"Will it be hard to watch?"

"Do you mean, will she struggle?"

"Yes."

"Unlikely. It'll seem like she's sleeping, except she'll stop breathing. Her heart will eventually stop, and she'll pass away."

He nods, and relief shows on his face.

She reaches out a hand and pats his shoulder, then they walk away, leaving him alone in the hallway. He takes a deep breath, then reenters the waiting room. My four boys are there, spread over two couches, as well as my sister, her husband, and my father. They all look at James expectantly when he enters. Grace is between Reed and Gilbert. Steve is beside Donovan as James stands before them.

"Boys, I just talked with the doctors. They did another examination of your mother. They said there's no change. They give her no chance to live. Although it's a very hard decision, we've decided to turn off her machines."

The room is silent, aside from the soft ticking of the clock on the wall.

"What does that mean?" Gilbert asks.

James looks over at him. "It means that it's time to let your mom go. She can't breathe on her own and never will again. We can't leave her rotting in a hospital bed. She's let go. Now we need to."

"What will happen?"

He exhales. "Her heart will stop and she'll die. But it also means she'll be free. She won't remain in her broken body."

Grace has her arms around the shoulders of both boys and hugs them to her. David and Donovan look away.

"We're all going to go down to her room. We can say goodbye and stay while they turn off the machines." He looks at each of the boys. "Any questions?"

"Will she feel any pain?" Donovan asks.

James shakes his head.

Silence returns to the room, and after several seconds, James asks, "Are you ready?"

The family stands, and James escorts them out the door. They walk down the hallway to my hospital room. Dr. Mitchell and the other doctor stand outside the door. Ginger and another nurse stand beside them. Dr. Mitchell opens the door, and my family files inside. All the furniture has been removed other than my hospital bed. They look at me, my chest rising and falling with each pump of air from the ventilator.

"Take your time," Dr. Mitchell says to James. "We'll be waiting right outside."

She closes the door, and my family surrounds my body. Tears form in Donovan's eyes. He takes off his glasses and wipes at them. Grace sees it and goes to him. She stands beside him, rubbing his shoulder. It's the first time he's seen me since finding me beneath the balcony.

My father steps away from the wall. He walks to the bed and places his hand over mine. He leans down and whispers, "Goodbye, honey." He kisses my forehead, then steps away and retakes his place against the wall. I may have imagined it, but something about his touch felt familiar. As if I could remember it.

After a few seconds, Grace steps to my bed. She reaches out and brushes my leg, looking down at me. Tears cover her cheeks. A sob escapes her throat, and her husband steps forward, gripping her shoulders. He hands her a box of tissues, and she takes one, dabbing at her eyes. "I'm sorry," she says to me. "I should have been a better sister. I should have shown you more compassion." She leans forward and kisses my cheek, then steps back.

A spark ignited at the feel of her lips on my cheek. I felt it. For the first time in days, my body reacted to touch.

Nobody moves, they only look at me on the bed. Finally, David looks at James, then steps forward. He grabs my hand, and I feel the electricity from his touch. "I'm sorry, Mom. I miss you. I love you." He raises my hand to his lips and kisses it. Fire erupts from my fingertips. *He called me Mom!*

He steps back, then Gilbert moves away from James and comes to me. He looks down at me as tears roll down his face. He kisses my cheek and says, "Love you, Mom." He turns away and almost runs into James's waiting embrace. James engulfs him in a hug, and my cheek burns from the touch of his lips.

Reed steps forward. His eyes are puffy and red, but he fights for control. He leans over me and kisses my forehead, whispering, "Goodbye, Mommy." He turns away, going to James. James releases Gilbert and hugs him as he sobs.

After several seconds, Gilbert reaches for Reed, and they embrace. James looks at Donovan, but he stands still, unmoving.

"Don," he says. "Do you want to say goodbye?"

Donovan nods. He takes several tentative steps forward, looking down at me. He reaches out, and when he touches my hand, pain emanates from it. A searing heat. Tears roll down his cheeks. "I'm sorry, Mom. Please forgive me." He leans forward and kisses my other cheek. I swear my skin reacts even before he touches it. Electricity pulses down my body.

He steps back but continues to look at me. James comes forward and puts an arm around him. They stand that way for several seconds before James releases him and takes my hand. It no longer surprises me I can feel. What surprises me is the comfort. His hand in mine feels natural. As if our hands were made to hold each other's. He looks down at me with tears in his eyes and shakes his head.

"I need you, Ri. I've missed you, and now you're leaving me for good." He pauses and looks down at my hand, then back at my face. "Goodbye," he says, then leans forward and kisses my lips.

My mind recalls the other day, when he sat here in this room looking at photos on his phone. He kissed me with wedding cake smeared from eyebrow to chin. We were laughing, and he laughed. Nothing I've ever seen looked more real. More natural.

He steps away from me and looks around the room. Everyone is crying. In that instant, I realize how much I was loved. For the last several years, I've taken it for granted, yet they went on loving me.

James takes a moment to collect himself, then steps to the door. He opens it and motions to the doctors and nurses, then steps back. The time has come, and I can't stand it. I want to run. I want to go back to following the detectives and learning about my life. I want to live. I want to return to my body and wake, but I know I can't. I've tried and something prevents me, almost as if a barrier exists between my body and spirit. I want to cry out as the medical professionals approach. Tell them to get back. I still don't know who tried to kill me. I don't know if my family will be better off without me, but I don't care. I want to be with them.

My family stands on the outside of the room, holding each other as they watch. I lie there helplessly as my life ends. The doctor switches off the ventilator and stands watching me. The other doctors and nurses step back and watch with my family.

My body shakes, and I wait for my chest to rise with air, but it doesn't. My surroundings grow foggy as I watch my body fade. I'm slipping away.

Chapter 40

No! I don't want to.

Something disturbs me. It rattles me, but I can't tell what.

Oh, I'm so tired. I just want to sleep. Leave me alone!

There it is again. Something's not right. What is that? I try to moan, but nothing comes out. I take a breath. It's shallow and feels like I can't get enough air. I take another and feel it again. It's somewhere else. Like someone is pulling on me. It's dark.

I push against my eyelids, and light bursts through them, then they shut again. I take a small breath and push again. They flutter this time. I don't recognize the room, but people are in it, surrounding me.

"Rita?" I hear an unfamiliar voice say. "Rita? Can you hear me?"

My eyes open again, this time longer, then shut. I don't recognize the face staring down at me.

"Rita, are you with us?"

A light shines in my eyes, and I shut them again.

"Rita?" a deeper voice says.

"Mom?" says another voice, more distant.

My eyelid is pulled open, and light bursts in my eye. I fight to close it but can't.

"Rita? This is James."

He has my hand. His touch is warm. I try to grip his back, but I can't move. My arms and legs aren't attached to my body. I push my eyelids open. James's face is over mine. He's looking into my eyes. A doctor is beside him. My kids are here too. They stand along the wall, watching.

"Rita, you've been in a coma. You had an accident."

I try to open my mouth, but I can't. It's as if my lips are glued shut. I look at him, trying to respond, but I can't.

He steps back, and the doctor moves forward. She looks into my eyes.

"Incredible," she says. She looks at the other doctor and the nurses. They all stand around me, shock in their eyes. She turns back to me. "Rita, my name is Dr. Mitchell. I've been your primary doctor since your accident. It's nothing short of a miracle that you've awakened. Are you in pain?"

I try to shake my head, but I can't. It seems I can only open and close my eyes. I have no control or feeling across the rest of my body. My eyes move away from her and search the room.

"I don't know if she can speak," she says to the other doctor. "Rita, your husband and four sons are here. Your father, sister, and brother-in-law are here too. Your accident was severe. You fell a long way and fractured multiple bones and experienced internal bleeding. We haven't been able to assess the damage completely. Can you move at all?"

Again, I try to shake my head, but nothing happens. Panic rises in my chest. I don't know if she can see me try. She watches me.

"Can she understand you?" James asks.

The doctor shakes her head. "I don't know. Rita, if you can't move yet, that's fine. It doesn't mean you won't. Your body is in shock. You've been asleep for a long time. It will take time for your body to recover and wake up."

I try to speak, but again, nothing happens. She watches me.

"Can you speak?"

I try to shake my head.

"Rita, blink your eyes twice if you understand what I'm saying."

I blink twice.

She smiles, and the nurse I don't recognize lets out a sob of joy.

"Rita," Dr. Mitchell says, "do you know where you are? Blink twice for yes, once for no."

I blink twice.

"Do you know what happened to you?"

I blink twice.

"Are you in pain?"

I hesitate. I don't know how to answer the question. I feel very little. My extremities feel disconnected from the rest of me. It's not really pain, but it isn't pleasant.

I blink once.

"Rita, do you recognize your husband, James?" She points to him.

I blink twice.

"And your children?"

I blink twice.

She turns to James. "Well, she appears to have at least some of her memory. Time will tell how much. But for now, this is extremely encouraging."

She steps aside and begins talking with the other doctor and nurses. One by one, each member of my family approaches. They squeeze my hand or pat my leg. I can't feel it, but I can see it. My eyes grow heavy, and although I fight it, I'm falling back asleep.

Chapter 41

Hank and Joyce

"Have you ever stayed overnight in a hospital?" Joyce asks.

Hank and Joyce sit on chairs in the waiting room.

Hank looks up from his phone. "I had a couple of semi-severe football injuries, but nothing that kept me in the hospital overnight. You?"

She nods. "When I had my son. I think it was three nights. I don't really remember."

"Was it here?"

"Yep."

He nods and looks past her at the door.

"What injuries?" she asks.

"In football?"

"Yeah."

"I broke a couple of bones in my hand my senior year of high school. In college at Boise State, I tore my ACL, MCL, and meniscus in my right knee."

"What happened?"

He sighs. "I got rolled up on. I got double-teamed by the right tackle and fullback. The halfback hit the hole and got knocked into me. He hit me just right, and my knee popped. I went down and knew it was serious."

"That was your junior year?"

He nods. "A year of rehab, but I was never the same. I had dreams of going pro, but I wasn't the same player after that. Six sacks my senior year, but I didn't get drafted. I had a tryout with the Philadelphia Eagles but got cut. The Vikings offered me a chance to join their minicamp, but I knew I wouldn't make the team. I declined and came back here."

Joyce looks at his leg. "Your right knee?"

"Yep."

"I would never know."

"I have a couple scars, but you haven't seen them. You never see me in shorts." He smiles.

"Lucky for me. Does it hurt at all?"

He shakes his head. "Not really. I worked hard in rehab. They've come a long way with knee repairs."

Movement outside the door grabs their attention. They can see heads in the hallway through the window. They stand and go to the door, opening it. The entire Burch family is walking toward the elevator. Smiles on their faces. Hank and Joyce look at each other in confusion, then follow.

"James," Hank says, "what happened?"

He turns around and looks at them with awe in his eyes. "She woke up."

"What?!" Hank and Joyce say in unison.

He smiles. "She woke up. They turned off the machines, and it woke her up. She was breathing on her own. She didn't die."

Hank and Joyce look at him open-mouthed.

"She's asleep again, but she's breathing on her own. She couldn't talk or move her body, but she was awake. She could understand the doctors' commands and blinked her eyes to respond to their questions."

Hank puts a hand to his cheek and looks at Joyce. Her mouth is open in shock.

"Does she remember anything about the accident?"

The elevator arrives, and the family steps on. "I don't know. She couldn't speak. She's asleep now." He steps onto the elevator. "Sorry, we're going to go celebrate." The door starts to close. "We'll come back later."

The door closes, and Hank and Joyce stare at the closed door.

"Wow," Hank says, cupping his hands over his mouth.

"Amazing."

"What now?"

Joyce shakes her head.

Two women in white coats pass, and one says to the other, "That's maybe the most amazing thing I've seen."

Joyce turns and says, "Are you Dr. Mitchell?"

The pretty woman with long dark hair nods. "Yes, but I have no comment."

Joyce shakes her head. "We're not press. We're the detectives investigating Mrs. Burch's accident."

Dr. Mitchell looks at them warily.

"We'd really like to talk with Rita."

"I'm afraid that's not possible. She's resting now."

"Does she have any memory of what happened to her?"

"We don't know. At this point, she can't speak."

"But you talked to her?"

"Yes, she could respond with eye blinks. I was only able to ask her yes-or-no questions."

"How long do you expect her to remain asleep?"

She shakes her head. "Hard to say. She's a mystery. She may never wake again, but after today, I wouldn't bet on it. She's a fighter."

"When she wakes, can we talk to her?" Joyce hands her card to the doctor. "Call day or night. It's very important we see her."

The doctor nods. "I'll let you know when I think it's appropriate for you to see her."

Chapter 42

Ethan

"Yes, sir. I get it. But the family won't speak to me."

Ethan Stone stands outside the hospital, holding his phone to his ear. The news director is on the other end of the call.

"This is huge. CBS National wants to go live with the update. This is your opportunity, Ethan. Find someone close to Rita. Someone you can interview live on air. If the family won't, convince them. You've got fifteen minutes before we break the news, with or without you. I'm counting on you."

The line goes dead, and Ethan looks over at Colby, his cameraman. "Did you hear him?"

"No, but I didn't have to."

Ethan nods, puts his hands on his hips, and looks up at the huge vertical EIRMC sign affixed to the side of the building. He knows this is his chance. It's a national story right here in little ole Idaho Falls and assigned to him. If he nails this opportunity, where could it lead? LA? Chicago? Miami?

He goes through his phone's call log.

"Who are you calling?"

He looks over at Colby and winks, raising the phone to his ear. After six rings, the voicemail picks up. He waits for it to end. "Erin, this is Ethan Stone from KIDK 3. I don't know if you heard, but Rita Burch is awake. I need an interview. Are you available? We can come to you."

He ends the call and immediately texts the number.

Rita Burch is awake. Need an interview. Will come to you ASAP.

Bubbles pop up on the screen then stop. He waits, watching the phone.

Erin?

No response. She's ghosting him. He looks up at Colby and blows out a breath.

"No-go?"

He shakes his head.

"What about the neighbor?"

"Which one?"

"The woman. Her best friend."

Ethan turns for the truck. "Let's go."

The two men jump in the news van and head for the Burch neighborhood, pulling away from the hospital. When they're out on the road, Ethan looks down at his phone. The news director is calling back.

"Yes, Bruce?"

"Do you have someone?"

"Yes, we're headed there now."

"James?"

"No. Kim, the neighbor and best friend."

"Couldn't get any of the family?"

"No, but Kim is almost family. She's as close as we're going to get."

"How soon can we go live to you?"

Ethan looks over at Colby, and he holds up a hand.

"Give me five minutes."

Jim ends the call, and Colby looks over at him. "What if she doesn't want to go on?"

Ethan shrugs. "Then I wing it. Ask forgiveness rather than permission."

"She might not be home," Colby says as he pulls into the neighborhood. They pass the Burch home and see nobody around. The lights are off at the Burch's. Ethan frowns, seeing his options for a backup plan are dwindling.

Colby pulls the van in front of the Long home and parks. Ethan jumps out and Colby exits, heading for his camera. When Colby comes around the back, Ethan is waiting for him.

"Go knock on the door."

Ethan shakes his head. "No, think about it. How much better will it be if we get her reaction live?"

Colby shakes his head. "Bruce isn't going to like that. We can't just go up to a house and knock on the door without telling them. You're going to get us in trouble."

Ethan extends a hand. "Think about it. It's like reality TV at its greatest. Rita's best friend learns about her waking up after she thinks she's died. Live, on TV."

Before Colby can respond, Ethan takes the microphone from him and jams the earpiece in his ear. He opens the broadcast signal.

"You got me?" he says.

A voice on the other end tells him they "copy." Ethan walks up the stairs to the entrance with Colby following. When they reach the landing, he turns, and Colby shoulders the camera.

"I hope you know what you're doing."

Ethan smiles and knocks on the door. He stands in the way of the doorbell camera so only black can be seen if someone scans the app. After several seconds, the porch light flicks on, and he sees Kim approach the door.

"Roll it," he says to Colby and smiles, holding the microphone as Kim Long opens the door.

Chapter 43

Rita

A series of beeps sound in my ears, and my eyes come open. It's dark in the room, other than the faint light streaming in from the window in the door. I can hear someone talking in the hallway, then the door opens. A woman enters the room in purple scrubs and white tennis shoes. She has long brown hair that's pulled back into a braid. She's in her mid thirties. I recognize her from when I first woke up.

"You're awake," she says, looking at me. She crosses the room and approaches the beeping machine. "Did this wake you? I'm sorry." She leans over the bed and looks into my eyes. "I understand you can't talk yet. Don't worry, you will. It will all come back."

I try to respond, but I can't make my mouth move.

"Are you in pain?" she asks.

I blink twice.

She nods and walks out of the room, then comes back and switches the IV bag.

"That should help."

We stare at each other.

"Would you like to watch TV? You've been all over the news."

I blink once.

"Okay. Well, I'll be back to check on you in a few minutes. One of the other graveyard nurses is celebrating a birthday today. They're serving cake in the break room. It's red velvet, my favorite." She smiles, turns to leave, then stops. "I'm Nicole, by the way. It's nice to finally meet you. I'll be taking care of you until six."

She exits, pulling the door shut, and I look at the clock on the wall. It's two thirty in the morning. I try to turn my neck to see out the window. My head doesn't rotate, but it flinches and moves ever so slightly. I take a quick breath and push with all my might. My head shifts about two inches. It's not enough to see out the window, but I feel an eruption of hope swell within me. Light streams on the bed, and I think it must be a full moon tonight. Either that or it's the lights in the parking lot surrounding the hospital.

A sound pulls my attention away from the window. My head moves back to the original position, this time with less effort. The door opens, and I expect to see Nicole, but it's not her who slips inside the door before closing it again. It's a woman. I can't see her face, but I can tell by her shape. She's wearing a black hoodie that covers her head, large pants, and sandals. She turns to me, pulls back the hood, and winks as my heart drops. She's come to finish me.

"Hello, Rita."

Panic rises in my chest. I fight to scream, but I can't. I lie on the bed, powerless.

"You just won't die, will you?" she whispers. "That fall would have killed almost anyone. But no, not the great Rita Burch. I couldn't believe you lived. When James called me and told me, I thought it was some sick joke. But then when I came to see you here, I was sure it was only temporary. You were so broken. The doctors were convinced you'd die. So was everyone else. But, again, you didn't listen. Even when they shut off the machines, you didn't die. You can imagine how shocked I was when the news reporter told me you were alive."

She approaches the bed but doesn't come to me. She unplugs the heart-rate monitor.

"We don't need the nurses being alerted to your death. Not until after I'm gone."

She reaches behind me and pulls one of the two pillows loose. My head thumps back on the remaining pillow, and sharp pain screams throughout my body. I fight to yell, but I can't as she stands over me, pillow in hand. Finally, a gurgling sound emanates from my lips.

She stops and grins. "What? Are you trying to say something?"

"Why?" I croak. It comes out little more than a raspy whisper.

She softly chuckles and shakes her head. "Of course you'd have to ask why. You don't get it, do you? It was all an act. The befriending you at the gym. The asking you for advice on my marriage and online business. I wanted you to believe I admired you. But you know what? I hated you. I hated the very sight of you." She leans down, inches from my face. "You're reprehensible. Everyone knows it. You're the kind of person who ruins this world. You're hated by those who claim to love you. Do you know that? Oh, sure, they admire your success. They might suck up to you because of your money. But they hate you, just like me." She frowns. "I have no idea how you did that, by the way. Luck, I guess. You aren't even that smart. Your success teaches people they can be awful to others, yet still be wildly successful. You're a scourge, and the world will be better off without you."

"Bob," I whisper.

"What about him?" She grins. "You think this is about him?" She shakes her head. "No, no. Bob is nothing. I never cared for him. He was just a little fun. This is about James."

My eyes go wide, but even the few words I've spoken hurt.

"Oh, yes. You don't know how good you have it. He loves you; heaven only knows why. He's a wonderful father to your boys. Compassionate. Loving. Easy to mold. And good looking. Everything my husband wasn't. Every day I'd see how he'd take care of you and the boys. And you were too caught up in yourself to see it. You didn't deserve him. He'd sit at Reed's basketball games alone. Or at Gilbert's concerts. He took care of everything and put his career aside to support you. Then you slept with Bob. I was disgusted when I saw you at that Shilo Inn welcoming him into your bed. You had everything, and now I'm going to take it—and James. I'm going to give him the woman he deserves."

She presses the pillow over my face. I try to take a breath, but it's suffocated in the padding. Panic rises in my chest, and my heart feels as if it's going to burst. I scream, but the softness drowns the sound as it's pressed against my face.

I've always wondered what it would be like to suffocate. To struggle for breath. To beg for oxygen and not get any. To know you will die. That's me now. I came back from multiple near-death experiences, but now Kim is finally going to finish the job.

A noise pulls my attention away from the pillow. A muffled voice asks, "What are you doing?" followed by silence. The pillow remains forced into my face. The pressure intensifies. Kim is pressing harder, driving my head deeper into the pillow beneath me.

"Get away from her," the female voice says, growing closer.

The hands release the pillow, but it stays over my face. I hear pushing and panting and know there's a struggle going on beside me. I can't see what's happening, and I can't breathe. I try to move my arms, to pull the pillow away, but I'm powerless. The lack of pressure allows me to push into the mattress. I'm not sure if it's working, except this time when I breathe, I get a small gulp of air. It's not enough, and panic rises again as I hyperventilate. I struggle again for another breath and tell myself to calm down. I struggle for peace as I listen to the scuffle beside me. Someone slams against my bed, and pain shoots through my body. My back and hip radiate pain.

"Step away from there," Kim screams. "No!"

An alarm blasts in my ears. Red light beams above me, so bright they radiate through the pillow.

"You stupid..."

A low thud, followed by the sound of a body toppling to the ground. To my left, I hear drawers being thrown open. Footsteps, and then the pillow comes off. Kim stands over me, a set of scissors in her hand. I scream as they fall toward me, and the sound of a gunshot ricochets around the room. Kim's body drops on top of me as the scissors slash down. Bolts of pain flash through the left side of my body where Kim has landed. Her hair covers my face.

The shuffle of feet and intense yelling.

"Get her off of her!"

Kim's body is pulled from mine as her hair slides over my face. A man in a security uniform holds her to the floor as Kim moans. A male nurse stands over me. A female nurse says, "I'll get the doctor," and leaves.

"Rita?" the nurse says. "Are you okay?"

My eyes leave him, and I see the scissors sticking up from the mattress, handles reaching upward. The points are resting deep inside the mattress beside me. Missing my body by millimeters.

Chapter 44

After the security guard and nurse took Kim from the room, Dr. Mitchell entered. She and Nicole, my nurse, stand over me. Nicole has a gash on her cheek, and she's favoring her right hand.

"Rita, can you hear me?" asks Dr. Mitchell.

"Yes," I whisper.

Her eyes go wide and she grins. "You can speak?"

"Barely."

Dr. Mitchell and Nicole smile at each other.

"That hurt."

Dr. Mitchell looks at me with concern. "I imagine. What hurts?"

"Everything."

"You can feel everything?"

"Everything above my waist."

"Can you move?"

I try to raise my hand off the bed, but that's too much. I wiggle my fingers, though.

"Very good," Dr. Mitchell says. "How about your toes?"

I concentrate my mind but don't feel any movement.

"That's okay. It'll come," Dr. Mitchell says, looking back into my eyes. "Do you realize how big a step that is?" She examines my arms and legs, then pulls my hospital gown up and investigates my body for injury. "You're lucky."

"Oh?" I ask breathlessly.

She smiles. "Even your IV remained in place." She rubs a finger over the spot where the scissors cut the sheets and mattress. "An inch to the left, and it would have been your liver."

I adjust my head to the right to get a better look when a shadow darkens the doorframe. The man is enormous, filling the entire doorway. Dr. Mitchell sees the shadow and turns around.

"This isn't a good time, Detective."

"I'd say it's a perfect time, Doctor," Hank Gardener says. He enters the room, followed by his partner, Joyce Powers. They both look different. Hank approaches the bed.

"We need to let her rest," Dr. Mitchell says.

"We're not going to ask her to run a marathon, Doctor," Joyce says. "She can stay right there in bed, but her testimony is critical to our case, and we can't wait any longer."

Dr. Mitchell looks at me, then at them, saying, "Fifteen minutes. That's all I can give you." She squeezes my hand then tells me, "I'll be back soon," and leaves.

I turn my head slightly so that I can see the detectives I know so well. They look a little different from this angle. The movement makes me gasp in pain.

"Rita, I'm Detective Hank Gardener, and this is Detective Joyce Powers. We're the detectives who have been investigating what happened to you."

"Okay," I say in a hoarse whisper.

"We'll do our best not to keep you, but it's very important we get your account of what happened. Is it okay if we record our conversation?"

"Fine."

"Good." He takes out a recording device. "Do you remember anything about your accident?"

"All of it."

"Do you remember why you fell?"

My speech comes out in halting breaths. It's agonizing to speak this much, but liberating as well. "I was walking onto the balcony. I had my laptop in one hand and was trying to log in to a Zoom call. I slipped on something as I reached the balcony. My laptop flew out of my hand, and I reached to catch it when I almost toppled over the railing."

"You stopped yourself?"

"I did."

"But you fell?"

"I was pushed."

"By who?"

"After I caught the laptop, I turned and saw a figure coming toward me. It was Kim Long, my neighbor. I remember thinking how strange it was that she was there when she reached out and pushed me. I was already awkwardly leaning against the railing. My laptop went flying, and I fell onto my back."

"And you're sure it was Kim?"

"Positive."

"Do you remember anything after that?"

"Nothing you'd believe."

"I beg your pardon?" Joyce says.

I look at her. "My spirit left my body after I fell."

Joyce motions to Hank, and he turns off the device. "What?" she says.

"My spirit left my body after I fell. I didn't remember who I was, but I knew somehow the body was mine."

Hank clears his throat. "You're telling me you left your body and then came back into it?"

"Not immediately, no."

"When?"

"Right before I woke up."

He points. "Here? In the bed?"

"Yes."

"And you remember all this?"

"All of it."

"What did you see?" Joyce asks, crossing her arms.

"I saw James come home. I saw my body brought to the hospital. I saw the boys come. I even followed your investigations." My voice is growing stronger with the practice of speaking.

"Us? You followed us?" Hank scoffs.

"I did. I know it sounds unbelievable, but it's true, and I can prove it."

"How?" Joyce asks, raising an eyebrow.

I look at Hank. "You've won two Cokes from her in the last couple of weeks."

Hank grins.

"Haven't you?"

He nods. "How did I win them?"

"*Pour Some Sugar on Me* by Def Leppard and *Cold As Ice* by Foreigner."

Hank's mouth drops open, and he looks at Joyce. She stares at him, then narrows her gaze on me.

"How did you know that?"

"I told you. I know all about you. I followed you. I watched you interview Erin at the office, Kim at her house, and Steve at the dealership. You knew it was Kim. You just couldn't prove it. But now you can."

"How?"

"Because I woke up."

The corner of Joyce's upper lip curls into a grin.

"By the way, I'm with you, Joyce. If you're sitting watching the action flick with Sam, he should be happy with that. You shouldn't need to be paying attention."

Hank laughs and covers his mouth, then shakes his head. "Incredible."

Joyce looks at him, smiling, then turns back to me. "Do you know what people said about you?"

I frown. "I do."

"Was it true?"

I look at the window. "Yes." I see her nod out of the corner of my eye.

"That's remarkable, but we need you to keep it to yourself."

I redirect my eyes to her. "Why?"

"Because out-of-body experiences are hard to explain. Especially to the prosecutor or a judge. It would be better for our case if you simply said what happened to you before the accident and again once you woke here in the hospital. In your body. Your credibility depends on it and our case."

I know she's right. If I hadn't experienced it myself, I wouldn't believe me either.

"I understand."

"I think that's enough for today, don't you?" she says to Hank.

He nods.

"I'm glad you woke up," Joyce says. "You're certainly a survivor."

"Destiny's Child."

She had turned toward the door but stops and looks back. "What?"

"You owe me a Coke," I say.

Hank laughs and claps his hands. "You're really paying out," he says to Joyce.

She rolls her eyes and walks out the door, but Hank remains watching her. Once he's sure she's out of earshot, he turns back to me.

"You probably know this already if you really were following us around. I jacked up my knee pretty bad my junior year."

"At Boise State."

"Right. That year of rehab sucked. I almost quit several times." He looks me in the eye. "That was nothing compared to the work it's been to get Saundra to trust me again." He nods. "Your rehab is going to be ten times worse. But James..." He shakes his head. "Do you feel me?"

It's not by much, and if he wasn't a detective, he probably wouldn't have seen it, but my head moved up, then down, ever so slightly.

Chapter 45

Dr. Mitchell comes back in and talks to me, but I'm so tired I can barely stay awake. I can see she wants to ask me something, but she stops herself and tells me to get some rest while closing my door. Before it even shuts, I feel myself fade.

When I wake hours later, sunlight streams through the window. My sister and my father sit in the chairs near the wall, softly chatting. I move, and they look up, seeing I'm awake.

"Sorry," Grace says. "Did we wake you?"

"I don't know," I say.

"I'll go get James," she says, rising to her feet.

"No," I blurt more forcefully than I intend. She stops. "I'm glad both of you are here. I want to talk to you." They look at each other. "Can you come closer? It's hard for me to talk loud enough."

They slide their chairs up to the side of my bed and look at me curiously.

"Dad, I owe you an apology." His eyes were down, and he looks up at me. "I'm still mad at you for what you did to Mom. I don't think I'll ever be able to forget it. But I forgive you for it. I was wrong to not talk to you about it. I'm sorry."

Tears well up in his eyes, and he shakes his head.

"Will you forgive me?"

He nods and swallows hard. I do my best to smile, and a tear drops from his eye onto his cheek.

I look at Grace. "I've missed you so much," I say, and my voice catches.

She reaches forward and grasps my hand.

"I've missed you too, big sis."

I didn't know it was possible, but a tear runs down my face.

"I wasn't there for you when you needed me most. How is Rachel?"

The mention of her name brings tears to Grace's eyes. "She's doing okay. She's a fighter, just like her aunt."

I smile. "When can I see her? I've got a lot of making up to do."

"I'll bring her by."

"Please."

We look at each other, basking in the unity we've been missing for all these years because of my stupidity.

"Are my boys here?"

"Yep, they came with James. They're in the waiting room."

"Would you send Reed in to talk to me?"

"Of course."

Grace and my dad stand, but before they reach the door, Grace turns back to me. She reaches out and stops my father, turning him back to face me alongside her. "Rita?"

"Yes."

"Was it you?"

"Was what me?"

"The money."

"What money?"

"The money that was donated to my church. Did you give it to my church knowing it would go to Rachel?"

"I don't know what you're talking about."

Her eyes narrow on me, then she looks at our father and smiles. He looks at Grace, then back at me.

"You knew," he says.

"Knew what?" I ask.

"Knew James was giving me money."

"I don't know what you're talking about. Now go get my boy, okay?"

Grace smiles and clicks her heels together just like she used to do when she found me a bossy older sister when we were teenagers. "Yes, ma'am," she says, saluting, then walks out of the room.

Chapter 46

Less than a minute after Grace and my father left, Reed poked his blonde head around the corner of the open doorway.

"There's my buddy," I say and motion for him to come closer.

He tentatively enters the room. He's thirteen and will pass me in height in the next year, just like his older brothers. "Are your dad and brothers all in the waiting room?"

He nods.

"Come here. Come hold my hand."

I reach for him and surprise myself when my hand actually raises. The movement removes some of his reticence, and he stands beside the bed and grips my hand.

"You aren't cold now."

"I was before?"

He nods.

"Were you scared?"

He nods again.

"How's basketball going?"

He shrugs. "I missed our game yesterday. We lost."

"Because they didn't have you?"

He grins.

I smile at him. "Reed, I'm sorry I didn't make it to all of your games."

"It's okay."

"No, it's not. I should have been there. I'm going to try a lot harder to not miss any. Okay?"

He nods.

"I love you, and I haven't done enough to show you. I'm going to do better."

He grins. "Mom?"

"Yes?"

"Are you going to come home again?"

His words cut me to the bone, and I have to swallow before responding. "Definitely. I don't know how soon. That's up to the doctors. But I won't stop fighting until I'm totally recovered."

He nods and smiles.

I squeeze his hand as much as I can. "Can you tell Gilbert I want to see him?"

"Sure." He turns to leave, but stops. "Mom, I'm so glad you woke up."

"Me too."

He leaves, and I try to raise my hand to my face to wipe the tear on my cheek, but I can't. My arm doesn't bend at the elbow.

After a few seconds, Gilbert enters. He's fourteen and will be in high school next year.

"Hey, Mom."

"Hey, buddy."

He stands awkwardly in the middle of the room.

"Come here. I'm injured, not sick. You can't catch it."

He smiles and comes forward. I reach out, and he takes my hand.

"How's rhapsody going?"

"Pretty good. I had a solo at the last concert."

"When was that?"

"Last week."

"Oh, I'm sorry I missed it."

He shrugs. "It's okay."

My face becomes serious. "Gilbert, I haven't been a very good mom recently, and I'm sorry. It wasn't you; it was me. I lost sight of what mattered. I promise you, I'm going to try harder and be better."

He smiles. "Promise?"

I smile at him. "If I could cross my heart right now, I would."

"I could cross it for you."

I have to swallow again and fight back the tears. I nod, and he leans forward, making a cross over my heart. His smile grows. "You will."

"You bet I will." I squeeze his hand, and we stare into each other's eyes. "I love you."

"I love you too, Mom."

"Will you go get Donovan for me?"

He nods and winks at me, then leaves the room. A minute later, Donovan comes through the door but keeps his distance.

"Come here," I tell him.

He doesn't move.

"Donovan, it's not your fault I'm here." I can see he's fighting back tears. "Honey, you didn't push me, and your dad got there right after. You were scared. You can't blame yourself."

He frowns and looks out the window.

"Honey, come here."

I raise my hand to him. Something about the movement changes him. He comes forward.

"Give me your hand."

He hesitates, but finally reaches for me.

"How's school?"

He shakes his head.

"You're struggling?"

He looks down and nods. I wait until he eventually looks up at me.

"How many weeks until school is out?"

"Three."

"For the next three weeks, after school, I want you to come here. Do you remember when you were little, before BEAU? We'd do your homework at the kitchen table in the old house."

He nods. "I liked that."

I smile at him. "Let's do it again. Every day after school, I want you to bring your homework. We're going to get you caught up. It won't be on the old kitchen table, but we need to spend more time together again. Okay?"

He smiles and nods.

"What do you think I'm going to say now?"

He gives me his crooked smile. "Get David."

I smile. "You're a smart boy."

He smiles bigger. "The smartest?"

I grin and wink at him. "Don't tell your brothers."

He chuckles and turns to leave, but I call him back.

"Donovan. I love you."

"I love you too, Mom."

He leaves, and within seconds, David enters the room. I look at him and once again can't believe how big he's become. He's strong and confident. I don't have to tell him to come to the bed. He stands right beside me, arms crossed.

"Hi."

"Hi," he says.

"Are you mad at me?"

He shrugs.

"You know what I think?"

"What?"

"You have every right to be."

My response surprises him, and he looks at me skeptically.

"I've let you down. And I'm sorry."

His expression softens, but he's still cold. "No offense, Rita, but actions are stronger than words."

The response hurts, but it's fair. "You're right. I'm going to prove it to you."

We look at each other for a few moments.

"Do you remember, a few years ago, when we went to California?"

He's unsure where I'm going with this.

"Remember that day at the beach?"

"That was fun."

"Do you remember when I buried you in the sand so only your face was showing?"

He chuckles. "Yeah."

"Let's do that again."

He looks at me, gesturing to the bed.

"Not this second. But I promise, as soon as the doctors say I can, let's go to the ocean and play on the beach."

He smiles. "Okay."

"But let's step it up a notch."

"What do you mean?"

"I mean, let's go to the best beaches. Let's go to Hawaii."

He swallows. "Are you serious?"

"Totally." His smile becomes a grin, and I chuckle, but it hurts. "Shake on it?"

He reaches out to me, and tears spring to my eyes.

"David, I love you."

He looks at me and nods. "I love you too, Mom."

We stay that way; me lying in the bed with him towering over me, holding my hand.

"Only one person left."

His face falls. "Mom?"

"Yeah."

"He won't come."

"He said that?"

He nods. "He's mad. He won't say what it's about, but I've never seen him like this. He's not angry. He's...hurt. I don't know what it is. What happened?"

"Go try, will you? Tell him he needs to talk to me."

David's jaw sets. "Okay, I'll get him."

He releases my hand and walks out, but two minutes later he comes back shaking his head. "He won't."

"Is he still in the waiting room?"

"Yeah."

"Okay, I need your help."

Chapter 47

"What are you doing?" Nicole, the nurse, says to David as she stands in the doorway. "You can't do that." She comes forward to stop him.

He's a head taller and at least fifty pounds heavier, but her reaction makes him take a step back. "Mom told me to."

"That's right," I say from my hospital bed.

David had released the brakes from the wheels on the bed and moved behind me, preparing to push.

Nicole looks at me. "You can't leave."

"I'm not. I'm going down the hall to talk to my husband since he won't come to me. Just to the waiting room."

She frowns. "The waiting room? This bed won't fit in there." She shakes her head and pushes the brake back in place with her foot. "No, you aren't doing this."

"David," I say, looking up, trying to find him.

He steps forward.

"Wait in the hall for a second, will you?"

"Sure."

He leaves and closes the door. Nicole and I stare at each other, neither willing to bend.

"Are you married?" I ask her. I know she is. I can see her left hand.

"Yes."

"Do you love your husband?"

"Most days."

I smile. "Fair. Have you ever hurt him? I'm not talking about mentioning how he's getting fatter or something like that. I mean, *really* hurt him. Messed up badly. Have you ever?"

She shrugs.

"Now multiply that by a thousand, and you'll know how I feel. If I don't talk to him today, I might lose him forever. I'll lose my family. I'll lose everything. I have to go to him. I have to show him how much he means to me before it's too late. Do you understand?" I can see from her expression I've reached her.

"You can't just have your son go wheeling around the ICU."

"Then you take me."

She shakes her head. "I can't take you. You can only be moved with a doctor's orders."

"Then get Dr. Mitchell in here."

"She's gone."

"Who's my doctor then?"

"Dr. Allen."

"Then get Dr. Allen."

She sighs. "You tried to get James to come?"

"I asked David to tell him to come. He won't."

"Just wait. Let me try."

She turns for the door, but I call after her.

IDAHO FALL   271

"Nicole, I've got to talk to him, or what was the point of me waking up? It's that important."

She nods. "I understand."

She opens the door and leaves. David comes back in.

"Mom?"

"The nurse thinks she can get your dad to come. We'll see."

He looks back in her direction. "Should I go too?"

"No, you keep me company. I might still need your muscles."

He grins and comes to the side of my bed.

"Dad told me about the first time he met you."

"He did?"

"Yeah, he said he knew he loved you when you came to the restaurant."

"The one he was working at?"

"Yeah."

I smile. "Can you believe I did that?"

He chuckles. "It was pretty cool."

My smile fades, and I look from him to the doorway. James stands watching us. David sees him and looks at me.

"Thanks, honey," I tell him.

David nods and walks past his father, patting him on the shoulder. James smiles at him, then wipes the smile away as he looks back at me. David closes the door.

"There's something I need to tell you. I've never told you this before."

He glares at me. "Another secret? Another lover?"

The words hurt, but I deserve them. "No. It's about the first time we met. At the soccer game."

He frowns.

"I know you think that party was a coincidence. That I just happened to be there. But the truth is, I knew who you were before the game."

He grimaces. "No, you didn't. We hadn't ever met."

"No, we hadn't. But I saw you with your friend. I saw Trisha talking to him. I was drawn to you from the first moment I saw you. I set it up. I got her to invite you and your friend to the party. I played harder in that soccer game than ever before, hoping you'd notice me. I saw you in the stands. I set the whole thing up."

He scowls at me. "Why?"

"Because I loved you before I even knew you. That hasn't changed."

He shakes his head. "Bob Love? Really?"

"I know. I can't explain myself. I don't even know what to say."

"Did you love him?"

"Of course not. You know what it was? It was an escape. I let myself believe I was doing everything in our relationship. We weren't getting along, and he pursued me. I was flattered. I'm ashamed of myself."

He shakes his head. "I don't know if I can get over this."

"I understand. But can you try? Will you let me work to make it right?"

He doesn't respond.

"Can I tell you something? You might think I'm nuts."

He looks away from the window and back to me.

"When I was in the coma, I saw you."

"You saw me? How? When I was here?"

"No, at home. I know it sounds nuts, but I saw you. I was at home with you. You were in bed, and all I wanted was to be there with you. In bed with you again. You're the reason I woke up. You're the reason I'm still alive. Without you, I wouldn't have had the strength to come back. I need you, James. I love you."

He doesn't move. He's perfectly still. But something in his eyes changes.

"I know it's going to take time. As long as it takes. But let's fall in love again. Let's fall just like we did at Idaho State. I promise you; nothing will ever be more important than you."

He looks at me and his Adam's apple bobs.

"Come here," I say and reach for him.

It's slow, hesitant, but he takes a step forward. He looks me in the eye and continues until he's reached me. He takes my hand in his. "I've missed you."

"Oh, honey, I've missed you."

"Not just in the coma. I've missed you for a couple of years now."

"I know. The missing is over."

Chapter 48

Hank and Joyce

Hank raises his eyebrows to Joyce in a "here we go" expression and pushes open the door. The room is void of color, with gray cinderblock walls and a table bolted to the floor. Kim sits behind the table, her attorney to one side. Her hair is pulled back in a braid, and she wears no makeup. Her right arm is in a sling. She's wearing a light-blue prisoner's uniform.

Her attorney is a wiry fortyish man with thin glasses and short brown hair. He stands as the detectives enter the room. Kim remains seated, her hands and feet shackled.

"Mr. Atkinson," Hank says, extending a hand.

Atkinson takes it, then shakes Joyce's hand. The detectives sit down across the table from attorney and client.

"My client is willing to aid you in your investigation for the deal I discussed on her behalf with the prosecutor. Mrs. Long is familiar with the deal and has agreed to answer your questions. I'll be here to provide her counsel."

Hank nods and opens the file he's held since entering the room. "Mrs. Long, thank you for your cooperation."

Kim says nothing, watching both detectives.

Hank removes the cap from his pen and makes a note on his legal pad. "You understand this discussion will be recorded and you consent to being interviewed and recorded?"

Kim nods.

"Please answer audibly."

"Yes."

"Good. Mrs. Long, how did you know the victim, Rita Burch?"

"We were neighbors. We went to the same gym. Our sons played on the same basketball team together."

"Okay. Tell us about the morning of Rita's fall."

"What about it?"

"You tried to kill her, didn't you?"

Her attorney, Mr. Atkinson, raises a hand. "Detectives, Mrs. Long has agreed to tell you what happened. Not what she was thinking about."

Joyce looks at him, then at Kim. "When did you first enter the Burch home?"

Kim looks at her. "Rita and I often went to the same workout class at five-thirty in the morning. I knew she'd be leaving for the gym around five fifteen. She never locked her car when she was there."

"At the gym?"

"Yes. After she got out of her car and went in, I switched my garage door opener with hers. It was the same brand. The openers looked identical. I drove back to the house, opened the garage, closed it, went upstairs, and silenced James's phone."

"Why?"

"Because I didn't want him to wake up the kids. I wanted them to all be running late. That way, when Rita got home, she'd be occupied with getting them ready for school."

"So that you could do what?"

"Well, after turning off James's phone alarm, I went home, got my kids ready for school, and told them I had to get ready for work. I snuck out of the house and went back to Rita's. I snuck in while James and Rita were arguing. I went upstairs, covered the balcony floor with starch, and hid behind the doors to the balcony."

"How did you know she'd go out there?"

"I watched her for a week. Every day after sending the kids to school, she'd go on her balcony and work on her laptop. I figured if she fell from the balcony, nobody would ask questions."

"Except she didn't fall."

She sighs. "She almost did. I almost didn't have to do anything at all. She slipped and slammed into the railing but didn't go over."

"That's when you came forward and pushed her?"

She nods.

"Please give your response verbally."

"Yes, that's when I pushed her."

"Then what?"

"I thought she was dead. She wasn't moving. I started to clean off the balcony, remove the starch, then her son came home."

"Did he see you?"

"I'm not sure. I don't think so. He was in the backyard. He got close to her body and then ran. I knew James would be home soon, and I had to get out of there."

"So, you left and went back home?"

"Yes, but James came home first. He didn't see me hiding around the corner. He came to the balcony, looked down, and saw her body. After he ran down, I replaced her garage door opener and snuck out the garage."

"You took yours, the one in her car, and put hers back?"

"Yes."

"Tell us about the hospital. How'd you get into her room?"

"I knew the code to the ICU."

"How?"

"My ex-husband is a doctor in the hospital. He kept a notepad in his office with passwords. I snuck in and found the passcode for the ICU. When I learned Rita woke up, I knew it was only a matter of time before she'd be able to talk. If she did and remembered the accident, she'd know it was me who'd tried to kill her. You two would finally have your evidence."

Hank and Joyce look at each other.

"Is that everything, detectives?" Mr. Atkinson asks.

Hank nods and closes the file. He stands, but Joyce remains in the chair. She and Kim stare at each other.

"I know you think it was about Bob. But it wasn't."

Mr. Atkinson puts his hand on the table and shakes his head at Kim.

"Oh, I know it wasn't about Bob. It was about money. She was a tremendous success, and you were a failure. You couldn't handle that."

"She got lucky."

"You know who says that? People who aren't successful. They always claim successful people are lucky. Maybe she was lucky, or maybe she was just a lot smarter than you."

Joyce gives her a half smile and stands, exiting the room with Hank.

Chapter 49

Rita

I turn off the TV and stare up at the ceiling. It's two a.m., and the hospital is quiet. It's been five days since I woke from my coma. I remain in bed. I have several fractures in my spine, one in my pelvis, and both my legs, along with my left hand. The doctors are encouraged, though. They believe I'll make a nearly full recovery. Everything but the use of my legs. I feel them, but I can't move them, and the prognosis doesn't look good. For the rest of my life, I'll likely be in a wheelchair.

Since waking, the doctors have pushed, prodded, and examined me. They've put me through multiple tests. My subdural hematoma has healed nicely. I had a concussion while comatose and when I woke, but now the fog has cleared. They believe I've suffered no brain damage, which I'm grateful for.

Dr. Mitchell said she can't believe I'm alive. The most fortunate thing about the fall was that I didn't break my neck. Had that happened, I would have died immediately. Instead, they plan to transport me to a rehabilitation center tomorrow. It'll still be like a hospital, but I'll begin my road to recovery. It'll also allow more flexibility with visitors. My family has been here every day since I woke, but only two can be in the room at a time. In the rehab center, we can all be together.

The door to my room opens, and it's Nicole. She's squinting into the darkness, seeing if I'm asleep.

"I'm awake."

She smiles and closes the door behind her. She wears a brace on her right hand. She pulled a ligament, fighting with Kim. She should take time off for recovery, but she says she can't until I've moved to the rehab center. I guess she kinda likes me and I like her. I'm so grateful to her and what she's done for me.

"How are you feeling? How's the pain?" she asks as she reaches the side of my bed. She's left the lights off, and I can only see her in profile with the light from the hallway behind her.

"I feel a little like I've been pushed from a balcony."

"Hmm, that's weird," she says, smiling. "Do you need me to give you something?"

"No, I'm okay for now. I don't like the way the drugs make me feel. I'll take the pain over the drugged haze."

"Okay, but don't be a hero. There's no need to suffer. They might help you sleep."

"If I'm still awake in an hour, I'll call you."

"It won't be me. I'm headed home. My shift is over. Tracy will replace me."

"Not Ginger?"

She turned her head to look at my IV bag and returns her gaze to me, frowning. "Ginger?"

"Yeah, the other nurse. The one with long red hair."

She shakes her head. "There isn't a nurse named Ginger. You've only had two nurses, me or Tracey. I don't even know of a Ginger who works in the ICU."

Now it's my turn to frown. "Are you sure?"

"Positive. Are you thirsty?"

"Yes."

She reaches over and gets my mug of water. Yesterday, for the first time, I could swallow on my own. I've never believed water had a taste until spending days without drinking any. The cool liquid tasted refreshing and smooth. It quenched my thirst in a way the IV bag never could.

I still can't get past her saying there is no Ginger. Ginger is the nurse I saw while in my coma. The one I saw talking to James and taking care of me. I know her name was Ginger. Or did I get the name wrong?

"Are there any redheaded nurses in the ICU?" I ask as she puts the straw of my mug to my lips.

"One, but his name is Danny, and he definitely doesn't have long, red hair. It's short. He's got a red beard, though."

Did I imagine her? If so, what else did I imagine?

I take a gulp of water and then another. A small amount catches in my throat and I cough. The movement makes my back and pelvis scream in pain. She pulls the mug away and watches me. I control the cough and take several deep breaths, calming myself against the pain.

"Are you okay?"

"I'm fine." I pause. "When I was in the coma, who came into the room?"

"It was several days. Your family multiple times, me, the doctors, Tracey."

"What about the detectives? The man and woman."

"Yes, them too. I think they were guarding you. They'd come in and talk for long periods. I think they thought your killer might try again." She laughs. "I guess they were right."

This news troubles me. I don't ever remember following them when they came into my room.

"Several times they sat in here talking alone. Just the two of them."

"About what?"

"I'm not sure. Once I heard them talking about your case. Another time I heard them discussing rock bands."

"Rock bands?"

"Yeah, they were talking about how he never knew any bands, but he guessed one right the other day while they were riding in the car." I raise my right hand to cover my mouth.

"What? What's the matter?"

I drop my hand, gathering my composure. I don't want to explain it. I don't think I could. "Nothing. It's nothing."

She watches me, waiting to see if I'll say more. When I don't, she says, "I guess this is goodbye. Since you're leaving in the morning, I'm finally going to take some time to let my hand recover."

We look into each other's eyes, and I wish I knew how to adequately express my gratitude to her.

"Nicole, thank you. If it hadn't been for you..."

She waves a hand. "I'm just glad I came to check on you. It was weird, like someone told me to. I don't know what it was. I thought I heard a whisper. A woman's voice. I'm glad I listened." She smiles. "I wouldn't mind a BEAU handbag. If you know anyone..."

I grin. "You've got it."

She reaches down and squeezes my good hand with her good hand. "I'm so glad you woke up."

"Me too. Don't be a stranger, okay?"

"You either."

She leaves the room and closes the door. I look back up at the ceiling in the dark. There's almost no moonlight tonight, and I can barely make out a ceiling at all.

Was it all in my head? Did I ever follow the detectives or watch James and the boys in the house? Did my mind create everything from the conversations I listened to while comatose? Is it possible that my brain made me believe I had an out-of-body experience when, really, I was here the whole time?

I shift so I can look out the window. *But it felt so real.* I knew things I couldn't know from simply overhearing conversations. They couldn't have talked about everything here. Then again, maybe my mind just filled in the blanks. Maybe I have more false memories.

And then I think of Ginger. I raise my right hand and place it on my cheek. My mother's name was Ginger. My mother had red hair. She was here. She was looking after me. My mom came back to take care of me. She told Nicole to come save me. I think back and know now it was her. She was teaching me what I'd become. She was showing me how I'd changed. She was helping me get back to who I should be.

I turn and look back up at the ceiling and ask myself a question. Does it matter? If I followed the detectives around or not? If I had an out-of-body experience? Either way, I learned who I became and what I needed to do. It wasn't just them who hated me. I hated myself. Everyone in my life deserved better than what I gave them. True, I've lost the use of my legs. But I've gained so much more. I've gained a new perspective. Now I've got a second chance, and I will not waste it.

Epilogue

A bonus chapter of this book is available for those who sign up to my newsletter. You can access the bonus chapter by clicking on the link below.

https://dl.bookfunnel.com/32fe2q6btb

Also by

D.J. Maughan

One Desperate Life

She's pregnant with his child when he deserts her...

Home in 1912 Chicago for the summer, Louise Clifford finds herself, once again, lost in the shadow of her more accomplished sister. When the alluring Texan, Charles Watson, pursues her, she clings to the lifeline he promises. However, after six weeks of bliss, he abruptly leaves.

Hurt and angry, she sneaks away in search of him. Finding him in his hometown of Austin, she's confused to learn he's answering to a different name. Now everything he told her back in Chicago is in question. She's trapped. She needs him but knows he's not the man she knew...

What else could he be hiding?

https://www.amazon.com/One-Desperate-Life-gripping-thriller-e
book/dp/B0CSH1L4VN

About the author

D.J. Maughan is an avid reader, event manager, father, husband, public speaker, and award-winning author. No surprise that he writes in the Thriller/Mystery genre, that's what he loves to read. He loves the unexpected and strives to provide that to his readers. He seeks inspiration everywhere, especially while studying and visiting diverse places and cultures. Whether jumping from a cliff in Hawaii or hiking the Plitvica Lakes in Croatia, he's in heaven as long as his wife and four sons are at his side. Learn more about him at djmaughan.com

Acknowledgements

Thank you to my beta readers. Your insights helped shape this novel. Brooke Maughan, Lupe Merino, Laurie Clark, Connie Maughan, Luke Barber, Matt Young, Jerry Paskett, Jim Thomas, Paul Gyorke, Kari Garrett, Laura Martin, and Debbie Altom.

A big thank you to my editor, Jonathan Starke.

Made in United States
Cleveland, OH
04 April 2025

15787447R00171